Produced by LouLou Productions LLC

Copyright © 2012 by David Carner

Cover design by R. Carner

EPUB ISBN: 978-0-9859514-3-6

Kindle ISBN: 978-0-9859514-4-3

Paperback ISBN: 978-0-9859514-5-0

I0681961

To find out more about John Fowler, please feel free to follow my author page on Facebook. The David Carner fan page currently holds all announcements pertaining to this series. Also check out www.davidcarner.com for information on this series and any other works. You may also follow me on twitter @davidcarner.

The John Fowler Novels

The Road to Justice

Sins of the Son

This Thing of Ours

Journey's End

Day's Past (Coming Christmas 2014)

Check out http://david-carner.blogspot.com/ for my free short story, Bad Day in Queen's Landing. The blog is updated with a new chapter weekly.

Dedication:

To my two girls: You two have been my rock. It's because of you that not only have I written a novel, but now I have written two. You'll never know what your love and support means.

To my many test readers and editors: Thank you for all of your help.

To you, the reader: If this is your first time to enter the world of John Fowler, then sit back and relax. I think you'll have a good time and a few laughs along the way. If this is your second excursion, then you know what you're in for. I can't thank you enough for coming back.

Chapter 1

John shook his head gingerly and checked his nose. Blood was freely flowing from it, or was that from his forehead? He really wasn't sure at this point; all he knew was that he was a bloody mess. John felt someone grab him by the leg and drag him behind a stack of boxes. As John turned to see who had saved him, he saw two of Bruce Cosby. "Great," he thought. "I'm seeing double." It was then that John's stomach rolled. He was nauseous, though he wasn't sure if it was from the blow he took to his head or seeing two of Bruce.

"You, okay?" Bruce asked. John couldn't quite make out what Bruce was saying. Either he had asked him if he liked hay, or if he wore a toupee. A shot rang out and hit the box over John's head. That, he heard clearly! John tried to remember how they got in this mess. It was all starting to slowly come back to him. Senator Jeremiah Cosby had been kidnapped. John and Bruce had tracked down the chief suspect, Luke McDonald, to this warehouse and were attempting to apprehend him. John and Bruce had found Jeremiah a few days earlier, and thought they had Luke cornered in this building. The only thing John knew for sure at that moment was Luke had pitched a grenade at John's previous location. The concussive force, and the shrapnel from the explosion, had about finished John off. If the boxes in front of him hadn't taken the fragment damage, John wasn't sure he would be here right now.

"Stay back," yelled Luke. "I've got a bomb and I'll take you out!"

Bruce sneaked a quick peek at the device.

"John," Bruce began. "I think if I were to shoot the bomb, it would go off and take Luke out without hurting us."

John stared at Bruce with amazement, put his finger in his ear and wiggled it around like he was trying to unclog it.

"I'm sorry; my hearing must be extremely jacked-up. I thought you just said you wanted to shoot a bomb!" John exclaimed. Bruce sighed.

"John, you're hurt and I can't take a chance of that maniac getting away and killing my father," replied Bruce.

"Bruce! He's got a freaking bomb! You have no idea what the payload is!"

"John, stay down," said Bruce. Bruce stood and took aim at the bomb.

"Don't, Bruce! I won't tell!" Luke yelled.

"You're right, you won't," said Bruce quietly where John couldn't hear him.

Bruce fired and John thought to himself, "Sam, I'm coming to see you a lot sooner than I planned."

The bomb exploded.

6 Days Earlier
New York FBI Office

Chapter 2

John walked into the New York FBI building. He was glad Trip hadn't taken away his FBI visitor credentials. John had to make a decision soon about what he was going to do. He currently was not a member of the FBI. He had been offered his old job back after assisting his former two partners, Chet and Jessica. Trip, the Director of the New York office, had offered the position and the file on John's wife's murder after the last case was over. John snickered. After the last case was over . . . that was yesterday.

He headed down the elevator to the foxhole. The name had always amused John. He had given the basement the name since most of the agents that had been stationed in the basement had dug in like they were in a foxhole; fighting for their careers. Not twenty-four hours ago, Chet and Jessica had been doing just that. Now, John had requested to have the three of them stationed there, permanently. There were a couple of reasons for that. The first was to try and stop the pressure that built up on the agents that were stationed in the basement when their careers were on the line. The other, well, it was simply to annoy Bruce. John knew by not only going into the foxhole and solving an unsolvable crime, but by also embracing the foxhole would just drive Bruce insane. If there was anything John went out of his way to do, it was to drive Bruce insane. John thought about the situation that he was about to step into. He smiled as he appreciated the irony. The elevator door opened and John stepped out.

As he headed down the hall he thought about his team. Well, they weren't his team anymore since he wasn't in the FBI. Chet was the computer guru. He could get information that John had no way of obtaining online. Truth be told, John could barely turn on a computer. There was also Jessica Hammerstein, "The Hammer." Jessica could get a confession out of anyone in interrogation. Then there was John. John had a way of finding a lead, or making a connection out of information that no one else seemed to be able to. Together, the three of them were an almost unstoppable force; that was until John left the FBI over three years ago, and became a private investigator.

John had been undercover for over a year within the Mafia. During that time he had succumbed to the lifestyle of the men he associated with and became an alcoholic. The night of a huge bust of alleged Mafia members by the FBI, John was heading home to tell his wife, Sam, that he was joining AA and would leave the FBI if she wanted him to. John had been thinking about how he was going to tell Sam his decision during his walk. He was yanked out of his thoughts as he got within three blocks of his apartment. The apartment exploded with Sam inside and John looking up at it after being knocked back by the explosion.

John had been a wreck since then. He barely remembered the funeral, or his interrogation ran by Jessica at the insistence of the FBI. What little he remembered about any of it was being drunk, and yelling at people. He yelled at his family and Sam's. He had only within the last week apologized to his family. He suspected Sam's family was still mad at him; he had just been served legal papers by them less than an hour ago. Sam's parents, Arthur and Madeline Moore, had filed suit against John in civil court for Sam's death. They were suing him for the trust Sam's grandparents had left to Sam which had been left to John after her death. John had no clue how much was in there. He just knew he had nothing to worry about moneywise for the rest of his life.

John came to the door of the foxhole and looked inside; there was Jessica. John smiled when he saw her and his heart jumped into his throat. It was strange; three years ago after John was interrogated by Jessica, he left the FBI letting her know that he hated her. For the next three years Jessica and Chet did all they could to solve the case of Sam's death. Jessica also kept John's parents and Sam's mother in the loop as to what was happening. Jessica ran interference for John after he blessed out a reporter when the reporter asked John about his late wife's death. In the past week John and Jessica had started to admit the romantic feelings they had for each other.

Jessica turned, saw John, and smiled at him. She motioned him in and John walked into the room. Inside the room were Chet, Trip, and Bruce Cosby. John and Bruce had a special hate-hate relationship. Bruce's father, Senator Jeremiah Cosby, had actually met John at Sam's house when John and Sam had first started dating. Jeremiah thought of Sam and John as the children he didn't have that he always wanted. Apparently Jeremiah, and Sam's mother, Madeline, had dated for a time before Madeline married her husband, Arthur.

Bruce and John's confrontations in the FBI had been legendary; with John coming out on top every single time. Bruce had actually asked for John on this case. This showed John exactly how serious the case actually was, and how serious Bruce was taking it. Jeremiah had been reported kidnapped a little over an hour ago. John walked up to Bruce and the room went quiet as Bruce turned to face him.

Chapter 3

"Agent Fowler," said Bruce, extending his hand. John reached out and shook Bruce's hand. It seemed like everyone in the room took a collective breath.

"I'm not an agent, Bruce," John replied with a slight grin. "I haven't made up my mind yet about what I'm going to do."

Bruce looked like he had been slapped in the face with John's statement. He turned quickly to the others and began to talk to them, when John put his hand on Bruce's shoulder. Bruce spun, with anger in his eyes. He looked loathingly at John's hand on his shoulder.

"Bruce, have I done something to upset you?" John asked.

"Have you done something to upset me? Have you done something to upset me? I need an agent on this, John! No! Let me correct that! I need the best the FBI has to offer, and you are not FBI! You're a consultant! I want someone who is dedicated to this! If you can't even dedicate yourself to the FBI then how can I know you will dedicate yourself to finding my father? Huh? How, John? How?"

Bruce turned; his face furious. Trip looked at John, shrugged and turned his back on John to help Bruce. Jessica mouthed the word, "Sorry," and went back to helping Bruce. Chet looked at John very uncomfortably. John nodded to his friend and Chet turned to help Bruce as well. John stood there for a second letting it all sink in.

John was the outsider here. There was no denying it. He knew he had to make up his mind right then. It was time to make the decision he had been avoiding. Did he walk away and let the FBI find Sam's killer and Senator Cosby's kidnapper, or did John cowboy-up and do what he was put on Earth to do? John knew he was the best chance they had of solving both cases, and he also knew he was the man with the best chance of finding Senator Cosby alive. He spoke very softly, barely above a whisper.

"Give me the papers to sign, Trip," John said. Trip froze. Bruce turned around very slowly. Anger was dying in his eyes.

"This isn't the time for one of our little games, John," replied Bruce. John shook his head.

"I'm not playing, Bruce. This is too important. I'm not ready for this yet, but your father's situation doesn't allow me that luxury right now." John turned to Trip. "Get me the papers to sign . . . I'm back."

John noticed Chet breathe a sigh of relief. Jessica's eyes sparkled mischievously. Trip had a tight lipped smile, which for him was the equivalent of a NFL wide receiver doing an end zone dance. Bruce offered his hand again. John shook it.

"Welcome back, John, and thank you," Bruce said. John nodded. "You have some papers to sign, John. I've left the entire file on my father with Jessica and Chet. The best I can tell, Secret Service Agent Luke McDonald is the last person to see my father. I'm going to leave now before my presence causes any problems. I have contacted Quantico asking for special permission to work this case, but I'm not expecting them to allow me any access. I don't know why not. John and my father are closer than the Senator and I are." John internally winced with the last statement Bruce made. Everyone was a little uncomfortable, and no one had any words of comfort for Bruce. He had spoken the truth and everyone knew it. Bruce left the foxhole and got on the elevator; as soon as the doors shut, the biggest grin in the world broke out over Bruce's face.

Chapter 4

Bruce walked upstairs to his offices. His team saw him and tried to console him. Bruce internally shuddered at the thought of having to be around this group of people. He stayed for just a minute and then began to choke up. Bruce told everyone he needed some air and left. Bruce was trying to hurry out of the building, but not appear that way. What John and company were not aware of yet, was Senator Cosby had been missing for over 18 hours at this point. Bruce made it to his car without being stopped. He left the FBI building and pulled out into traffic. He drove a bit and pulled into a parking garage. Bruce drove up to the top of the garage, and parked the car. From where he was, he was within a stone's throw of the river, and he could look out over the city. Bruce reached into his coat, pulled out a pair of gloves and put them on. After he made sure there was no skin exposed, he reached into the glove box and pulled out a cell phone. There was one number preprogrammed into the phone. Bruce dialed it.

"Go ahead," the voice on the other end said.

"John Fowler is back in the FBI like you requested. I have currently pulled myself off of the case. I have told his little group I am waiting for permission from Quantico. You might want to contact those you know there to get me back on the case so I can report back to you. The group is about to begin questioning McDonald . . . do I need to do anything?"

There was a pause; Bruce began to wonder if the phone call had been dropped. The voice on the other end finally answered.

"Not at this time, but if I do need something, it will be for you to take care of the situation permanently . . . will that be an issue?" Bruce laughed.

"Why would that be a problem? Anything else?" Bruce asked.

"No, I'll take care of Quantico," said the voice on the other end. "Bruce, if you double-cross me."

"You'll never see it coming," interrupted Bruce. "Look, I have no want or reason at this point to do anything to you. As I told you last night, I have my agenda . . . you have yours. One last thing . . . ARCHIBALD," Archibald hissed in anger. "You mention me to your other mole, I'll make sure you go down and your lovely daughter does as well." Bruce hung up the phone before Archibald could retort. Bruce got out of the car and looked out over New York City.

Chapter 5

Bruce thought back to the events that had taken place yesterday. Lisa Sparks had been arrested for her part in the death of Beth George and the attempted murder of David George. The murder and attempted murder had taken place over 25 years ago. Bruce smiled when he thought of Lisa; here was a woman after his own heart. She did what was best for her. She could care less about what happened to anyone else, well, except for her father, Archibald. Lisa's real name used to be Veronica, but she had it changed after the murders. Lisa had found herself taken hostage when David George, the kid she had tried to have murdered years ago, decided to get revenge over the murder of his sister, Beth. Bruce laughed silently, he really admired Lisa.

His mind then took him to thoughts of David George. Bruce really hated him. John had been out of the FBI until David's little murderous rampage over those that were involved, or had helped cover up the incident in Kentucky, brought him back to the FBI. Bruce really didn't want John back in the FBI, but the last thing he wanted was John being a consultant. Bruce had rather John stayed away and been a private investigator. If Bruce couldn't have that, then John needed to be an FBI agent. At least this way Bruce could know most of what John was involved with, and not arouse any suspicions. Bruce could always use the excuse of collaboration among agents, and all of that jazz. If John had remained a consultant, it would have been harder for Bruce.

Bruce reached into his coat pocket and pulled out a small cloth bag closed by drawstrings. He opened the bag and looked inside. He smiled as he pulled out the ring. It was a simple gold ring. Inscribed inside it simply read, "Always yours, John." Bruce replaced the ring in the bag, closed it and made sure it was securely tied. Bruce thought about his mother who had died at a young age. If his dad was to die due to these unfortunate circumstances, then he would have no family. This thought made him smile. Bruce chuckled to himself. He put the bag back into his coat pocket and spoke to himself very softly.

"If I had a sister, I wouldn't miss her."

The saying was a ritual he had since the first night he got the ring over three years ago. Bruce inhaled deeply. A sick, evil smile covered his face.

"John, John, John," he said softly to himself. "They say to keep your friends close and your enemies closer. Do you know why, Johnny boy?" Bruce opened his eyes. There was a look of pure hatred in them. "It's so you can find the perfect place to put the knife in someone's back."

Bruce stood there for a moment, thinking again about having no family. Bruce took the battery out of the cell phone, and then threw both the cell phone and the battery into the river. As he watched them both sink he decided he liked explosions and fire a whole lot more than drowning and water. Water just wasn't as fun.

Archibald Staples
Virginia

Chapter 6

Archibald stared at the phone like it was a snake that had tried to bite him. He had to give Bruce Cosby credit. The man was devious . . . Bruce was like the son he never had. Archibald laughed out loud at the irony of it all. Senator Cosby hated the way Bruce was and would have preferred John Fowler for a son, or John's late wife, Sam, for a daughter. Archibald was looking out over his land from the patio on the back of his mansion. It was quite chilly outside, but Archibald didn't care. He couldn't let a little thing like weather affect him.

He thought about John Fowler. Archibald wasn't thrilled with John being back in the FBI, but it was the best solution to a bad situation as far as he was concerned. If Archibald could maneuver Bruce to help him make it look like McDonald was a lone wolf nutcase, then John was less likely to look any deeper into the mess McDonald had caused. Archibald was counting on John's relationship with the Senator to concern John more with finding the Senator than worry about who was behind the abduction. With Bruce there . . . Archibald smiled for a second, he could find a way to eliminate McDonald. Archibald silently cursed his daughter for telling McDonald to contact him. Well, that was water under the bridge, time to move on.

Archibald looked behind him at the group in his office. The patio doors were shut to his office, but he could see thought the glass the lawyers that were crawling all over his office. Archibald really didn't like lawyers, but he wasn't about to spare any expense for his daughter. He had to take care of her. Archibald threw back his head and roared with laughter. That was great. That was the funniest thing he had heard in months and he had thought of it! Archibald caught his breath. It was time to be serious. Lisa shouldn't spend a minute more in jail than was absolutely necessary for one very important reason. She was the one person in the world who could give the authorities the information they needed to catch him.

Archibald truly believed there was nothing the authorities could pin on him without several different of his associates banning together to rat on him; Lisa however . . . well, she knew just about everything. Lisa would never tell anyone anything, but why take the risk. Archibald got one of his bodyguard's attention and had him come outside. The bodyguard brought Archibald a drink out on the patio to try and not attract attention. Archibald kept his voice low so he couldn't be heard inside.

"You do know who 'The Duck' is?" Archibald asked. The guard nodded. Archibald took a drink of scotch. "I need you to tell him something." The guard nodded. "Tell him I need to collect on the favor from three years ago; he'll know what it means. Tell him not to contact me; I'll get in touch with him." The bodyguard nodded and headed in. Archibald finished his scotch, and sat down the glass on the table on his patio. Archibald walked up to the doors and opened both simultaneously.

"All right, you overpriced crooks!" Archibald exclaimed. "Let's get my baby girl out of jail!"

John Fowler
New York FBI Office

Chapter 7

John watched Bruce leave the room and felt for
him. Whether or not Bruce and the Senator cared for each
other didn't really matter; what mattered was a man was
kidnapped and that man had a son. A son that John
loathed, but Bruce was Jeremiah Cosby's son regardless.
John felt everyone's eyes on his back and slowly turned
around to see the other three staring at him. Trip broke the
silence.

"John, if you're serious, I'll run upstairs and get the
forms," Trip said. John nodded. Trip turned to Jessica and
Chet. "Agents Chet Morris and Jessica Hammerstein, I am
going to team you with John Fowler if there is no
objection." John waited for Jessica to make a big deal out
of things. Chet was beaming. He seemed the most relieved
John had seen him since before Sam's funeral. John looked
over at Jessica. She had a coy smile on her face. John
raised his eyebrows at her in question.

"No objection, sir," said Jessica quietly. Chet shook
his head no and Trip took off for the paperwork. John
turned and pointed to the monitor and Chet began to do his
computer thing. Chet was unbelievable when it came to
operating a computer. John had said many times that Chet
could have been a great developer of programs, a hacker, or
both. John looked at Jessica. She was known by the
moniker "The Hammer". If Jessica got you into
interrogation, then your best hope was to tell her everything
you had ever done wrong in your life . . . and that your
story was consistent.

John remembered when the three of them had first started working together on a case. An old lady had been housing a terrorist, unbeknownst to her. The lady was having trouble keeping her story straight because she was simply forgetting details. Trip was worried Jessica was going to induce a heart attack in the lady before they cracked the case. John had always found Jessica interrogating people funny until he received the full treatment after his wife's death. He had never asked how long Jessica had questioned him, he had heard for two hours, but he was sure it was at least a week and a half.

The computer screen flashed up and John turned his attention to it. John scanned the screen, all of the information he already knew. John picked up the file. There was nothing in there. It was time to talk to Luke McDonald. He turned to Jessica.

"Is there any reason we should consider Luke as a suspect?" John didn't want this investigation to get off on the wrong foot, but he didn't want to turn Jessica loose on the man when he could be the best chance of leading them to the Senator, if he were the kidnapper. Jessica smiled; she knew exactly where this was leading.

"No, John," she said simply. "Look I have a little paperwork to finish up over the kidnapping yesterday, so why don't you go talk to him and I'll finish this up. You find something you don't like or question," Jessica got a sadistic grin on her face; John shuddered. "Then I'll take a run at him." John started to go. "John, wait." John turned back around. "You should probably know, I talked to prosecutors this morning, both Lisa and David will probably not serve any jail time. There is no real evidence to hold Lisa on, and she has the bestT lawyers money can buy. David's lawyer is already starting to work on a temporary insanity plea."

John looked very confused. He had expected that Lisa would use the fact she was held at gunpoint to give her "confession", but David's activities had been filmed; at least that what John had been told.

"How's that?" John asked. "Crazy or not, he killed four people in cold blood on camera." Jessica looked at him like he was crazy. "It was booked into evidence," John said looking at Jessica like she was crazy. Jessica had no idea what John was talking about. She went through the file and there was no mention of a tape or DVD booked into evidence of the mourners being killed. She looked up from the file, and looked at John. She acted concerned and checked John's head like he had a fever. She didn't move her hand as she spoke. "Hmm, you don't seem warm." She moved her hand onto his cheek. "You're heartbeat does seem a bit elevated," she said coyly.

John realized right then and there that either Jessica didn't know anything about the evidence he was talking about, or she was lying. Little things had been nagging at John since Jessica and Chet had approached John to return to the FBI. Inconsistencies in their stories, small ones, but inconsistencies none the less, had made John wonder if he wasn't missing something bigger. Something in John's head told him to keep all of this to himself. This ran through his mind in less than two seconds. He realized he needed to respond to Jessica's coy comment.

"I was thinking about getting the meatloaf from the cafeteria," John said trying to gauge Jessica. "It's probably the best meatloaf I've eaten other than my Mom's." Jessica rolled her eyes. "That's probably what caused my heart rate to spike," John replied, smiling. "Or it could be the gorgeous lady I see standing in front of me." Jessica smiled warmly. John looked over Jessica's shoulder at Chet who was in his own world. He had his ear phones in, working on the computer. "Chet!" John yelled. Chet turned around and saw the two of them together. He apologized and ran off thinking they wanted some time alone. John thought about going after him, but something was gnawing at the back of his brain. This might be the perfect time to question Jessica without Chet around. Jessica dropped her hand from John's face.

"What are you thinking, John?" She asked.

"Isn't there a video or DVD listed in the evidence?" John asked. Jessica rechecked her paperwork twice and shook her head no. John smiled. "You know I may have been dreaming that. I probably was. It was early on when we first started this thing that I thought I heard it. I'm sure I just imagined it." Jessica nodded and looked at John strangely. "I'm fine Jess; it's just been a lot the past few weeks." Jessica smiled warmly at John. He turned to head down to the interview rooms. John's mind was spinning. Did someone simply not file evidence? As bad as that would be, it would be better than what John was suspecting; there was a mole in the FBI. Worse than that, one of his friends was that mole.

As he was walking toward the conference room where Luke McDonald was, he saw a door open to one of the interview rooms and inside sat David George. John stopped, looked around, and saw no one. John opened the door and stepped inside.

Chapter 8

As John stepped inside the interrogation room, the man who John could only assume was David George's lawyer, stood up in outrage.

"Who are you and what are you doing here?" the lawyer asked. David touched the lawyer's arm to calm him. The lawyer turned to David.

"Relax," David said. "This here is one of the good guys," pointing toward John. "John, this is Tom Evans, my lawyer. Tom, this is John Fowler; the man who saved my life." John did what any good boy raised in Kentucky would do, he extended his hand. Tom took John's hand and shook it, a little suspicious. After they shook hands, John sat down. Tom remained standing. David laughed at his lawyer.

"David," began John. "I can use your help. Senator Cosby has been kidnapped and there are a few things that are inconsistent. I'm just trying to find out some facts to save his life. He was one of the ones who helped me find out things about Veronica, David."

Tom was ready to make a deal, shout "don't answer that", and several other things all at once. David motioned for Tom to sit down. David nodded for John to go on.

"Two questions," said John. John looked at the lawyer for a second and then began. "When you allegedly shot four mourners," John paused to make sure everyone was ok with the phrasing of the question. The lawyer nodded and David just smiled. John smiled and continued. "Allegedly, a video was sent in by the killer." David looked very confused. He thought a second before he answered.

"I don't know what the killer of those four mourners did, but if it was I who committed that act all I would have done was leave the note about Veronica." David's answer made John smile. Tom was about to have a conniption fit over what his client had just said. John nodded.

"Second and final question, do you know anything about the kidnapping?" John held his hand up before the lawyer exploded. "The ONLY reason I ask is the short amount of time between you taking Lisa hostage and Senator Cosby being kidnapped. There was roughly 18 hours in between the two events." David shook his head.

"Mr. Fowler, I know nothing about any kidnapping." John nodded. He didn't think he would be that lucky. "That's funny though, "David continued. "If you were going to kidnap someone, wouldn't you do it while everyone was distracted with what was going on in the White House?" John looked at David. John's stomach sank. That was the most logical thing John had heard about this kidnapping yet, and if it were true then that meant that Jeremiah had actually been gone closer to eighteen hours rather than one or two! John thanked the men as he bolted from the room and headed to the conference room where Luke McDonald was.

Chapter 9

John looked through the window at Luke McDonald. He had read the file on Luke, and didn't like what he had seen. Luke had come up with the handle for the first lady, Veronica Nichols. Luke had given her the handle "Silk". There was something that just didn't sit right with John about the name. Senator Jeremiah Cosby, the man who had been kidnapped, had told John, Trip and the rest of the team that someone in the White House had sent a Secret Service man to meet with him the night before Senator Cosby was kidnapped. When John and the Senator had landed in DC yesterday after their helicopter flight, the man John was staring at, Luke McDonald, was the man who had ran up to the senator. It was time for John to get the full story.

John took a deep breath and opened the door. Luke stood up and offered John his hand. John smiled at Luke and shook his hand. John offered Luke a seat. When both men were sitting, John leaned back. John wanted to make sure Luke was very comfortable.

"Luke, I'm sorry to take so long, I'm just getting up to speed on this case myself." Luke nodded with a tight smile. John continued. "So let me make sure I understand what happened. The Senator and I landed in DC, and then you two took off to work on another way to end the standoff." Luke nodded. John pretended to glance back into the file. He looked at Luke and continued. "So what happened next?"

Luke looked very confused as he answered. "I don't know; that's when I got knocked out." John leaned forward. Luke looked nervous. "Do I need a lawyer?"

John waved his hand. "Now why would you want that, Luke, I'm just asking what happened. This is all new to me." Luke looked a little perturbed.

"You realize you're wasting precious time questioning me?" Luke was mad. "It's been nearly 20 hours since I last saw the senator. I'm going to assume no one has seen him since me!" John's stomach sunk.

"Why wasn't that notated in the file, Luke?" John asked.

"How would I know what Bruce did?" Luke retorted. John didn't move a muscle but inside it felt like he'd been slapped in the face. Bruce had questioned Luke and he knew. Bruce knew his father had been gone that long. One of two things were going on here. Either Bruce was in on this, or Bruce was in more grief than John knew existed inside of Bruce. Luke was waving his hand in front of John's face. John snapped back to the present.

"Okay, Luke," John said. "Let's do this from the top so I understand this. I know you've talked to Bruce, but apparently the grief has caused him not to properly notate the file." Luke nodded, but John caught the slightest hint of relief in Luke's face. John was absolutely positive that Luke had something to do with what was going on . . . proving it might be a little more difficult.

Chapter 10

"You and the senator landed," Luke began. "I was hit with a stun device after the senator and I walked over to the other parking lot so we could talk in private."

"Why were you and the senator talking to begin with Agent McDonald, that's the part I don't understand?" John asked. Luke nodded. He scratched his face and looked around. He leaned forward like he was about to tell John a huge secret. John prepared himself so he wouldn't scoff in Luke's face. John was certain a two-ton pile of cow manure was about to come out of Luke's mouth.

"Archibald," Luke paused. "I mean Mr. Staples," John nodded. "Well, you see, he was worried about his daughter. All of those old friends of hers had been in the news the last few days. Mr. Staples was concerned about someone trying to hurt her, or even blackmail her. He was afraid someone would look into her past and the terrible things that happened to her. And yeah, I was supposed to see if I could get Bruce on the case instead of you. Not because of anything wrong that had happened, but because Bruce understands." John raised an eyebrow. Luke thought for a second, searching for the right words.

"John, let's be honest, you didn't exactly come from the same stock of Bruce and Lisa," Luke paused a second. "I guess it's Lisa now," Luke said. John nodded begrudgingly, and smiled. Luke smiled, thinking he had given John enough information to back off looking in his direction. Luke continued. "I mean, come on, let's be honest. You married way out of your league. Those families are the upper echelon of society, John, and they all keep secrets. Heck if anyone understood the need for secrecy it's your late wife. Her old man, the senator, and Mr. Staples all ran in the same circles and they knew how to keep secrets."

John leaned forward, looking angry. He wasn't angry; he knew exactly what was being implied. John was smiling inside and slapping his head inside at the same time. Luke had screwed up and reminded John of something he had forgotten. The Moores knew more about the Staples than anyone else. Why John hadn't put two and two together he wasn't for sure. John knew what he had to do here to make Luke think he was off the hook. He took a deep breath.

"Luke, I follow 90% of what you are saying. However, there's about 10% I'm not sure I'm interpreting correctly. If I understand what you're trying to say, I'm currently looking for not only the senator, but you're implying he's my father-in-law?" Luke was looking very, very uncomfortable.

John continued. "I know there are many more similarities between my late wife and the senator than between Arthur and Sam, but if for a second I thought you were trying to insinuate that Madeline Moore, one of the finest women I have ever had the privilege of knowing," John's voice continued to rise as he spoke. Luke's back was straight up against his chair. John's face was growing redder by the minute. John continued.

"Had an illicit affair with one of the finest gentlemen this country has ever seen . . ." A knife could have cut the air. John sat down, rubbed his hand against his head, and then straightened his shirt. He had a very tight smile on his face. He spoke very softly. "I have no idea what I might do to someone." Luke gulped and nodded. John nodded and left the room. Luke exhaled as the door closed. As John stood outside the door he smiled. He wasn't The Hammer, but he got exactly what he needed out of Luke. John walked down the hall whistling.

Chapter 11

John was trying to go over everything in his mind, but too many things were running together. This bothered John. Not three years ago he could have separated everything into the exact compartment it need to be in, but that skill had apparently accumulated some rust. John would normally turn to his team to help him, but part of the problem was he thought that one or more of them was possibly involved.

John never had a lot of friends. Sam probably was his only true friend in life. Chet had become the closest thing John had to a friend that he wasn't romantically involved with. And then . . . then there was Jessica.

He could hear Sam telling him how he was looking for an excuse to not be hurt again. John stopped walking. He was in one of the hallways that were rarely used. He had come here many times in the past to pace and think. This time was different. He leaned against the wall and exhaled deeply. This was hard for John. He had only had one true romantic relationship in his life until now, and that was Sam. He and Jessica had always talked to one another, and John was always going on about how Jessica needed a man in her life. Jessica would always barb back with him, but neither of them would have ever have made a move on the other. It was always lighthearted and in good fun. Sam always used to warn John he was either going to get fired for harassment, or get beat up by Jessica. John would never dream of cheating on Sam. He honestly didn't even know he had feelings for Jessica until a few weeks ago.

John had heard the whispers his entire life about Sam being Jeremiah's daughter and John had promised himself he would never do anything to put Sam in the situation she found herself growing up in. Sometimes he wondered if the rumors and innuendo wasn't what killed Jeremiah's wife. Yes she died of cancer, but in the end she didn't seem to have the will to live. That was the time the whispers were the loudest. John hadn't been in Sam's life when all of that had happened, heck he wasn't even out of high school then. John wondered if that was why Jeremiah was truly the southern gentleman he seemed to be. Did all of those things that had happened in the past drive him to try and root out and destroy any traces of corruption?

John shook his head. He was getting off track, but in a way, all of this was related. He had a bad feeling building in his stomach. He wasn't sure if it was because he was afraid a member of his team was a mole, or that this case might lead him to have to talk to his in-laws, Madeline and Arthur Moore. John subconsciously touched the pocket where the summons rested. John had to talk to someone and straighten out all of the thoughts that were bouncing around in his head. He was afraid of what might happen if he did with the wrong person. John straightened himself and headed to Trip's office. This was not going to be pleasant, but John had to figure things out, now.

Chapter 12

John knocked on Trip's door. Trip was on the phone, arguing about something. Apparently Trip was being given marching orders, and he didn't look very happy about it. John scribbled a note and dropped it on Trip's desk. Trip hung up and looked at John. Trip set his jaw. John braced himself, it was about to be bad.

"There's been a development with your reinstatement," Trip said. John looked at the floor. This day just went from bad to worse. Trip continued.

"Apparently, Quantico thinks that you need a psychiatric evaluation and they think it might help if there was someone on staff here to take care of that. He's been in my office most of the morning. I've been trying to get clearance for this case, and then you have the evaluation, but the good doctor has gone over my head. I had Chet clear out things in one of the unoccupied offices downstairs."

Trip was holding something back, John could feel it. He was pretty sure what it was, so John decided to throw it out there.

"They want me to have regularly scheduled visits to make sure I don't eat a bullet?" John asked. Trip flinched at the words. John knew he could have said it much nicer, but why bother? John knew he would have to pass an evaluation at some point. To be honest, John didn't know if he would pass it or not, and frankly until today he didn't care. Trip looked John in the eyes. There was a steely glint in Trip's eyes. He spoke.

"John, no one here thinks you are suicidal. Prove me wrong and I'll kill you myself; understand?" Trip barked. John choked back a laugh.

"Why, Trip, I didn't know you cared," John said. Trip waved away the comment, disgusted. "So when I go to these sessions, what I say there is confidential and I talk about things, right?" Trip repeated back John's question to himself; knowing that John was up to something. They had been down paths like this many times. Trip eyed John with suspicion, but nodded.

"So where might the good doctor be located?" John asked, a smile covering his face.

"Down your 'pacing hallway'," Trip replied. "It seems that he saw you earlier doing one of your infamous 'thought walks'. He called me to let me know he was available. I called Quantico as soon as I got off the phone with him. I don't know why, but something just didn't sit right about him after the conversation," Trip shrugged his shoulders and looked at John suspiciously. "John, is there something I should know? You've been here less than an hour and you are already being requested by a psychiatrist. Quantico says you have to, but I can hold them off for a day or two if need be."

John smiled and pointed to the note on Trip's desk. "Man, I must be important," John said. Trip looked a little confused. "Quantico had someone here before I had even asked to be reinstated," John said, lifting his eyebrows twice. "I never have known Quantico to be that efficient, it almost seems like this was . . . planned," John said as he turned, and headed out the door. As he passed through the doorframe into the hallway, he spoke. "Is there anything you should know? Nothing to worry your pretty bald head over, Boss."

Trip unconsciously reached up to touch his head and growled. He looked at the note John had dropped on Trip's desk. It simply read, "Senator missing since we landed in Washington last night." Trip groaned, looked up at the ceiling and shook his head. He knew he needed John, but he needed John cleared for duty before John could do anything. If something went wrong with this high-profile case, and John wasn't cleared for duty . . . Trip didn't want to think of the political firestorm that would rip through the FBI. Trip started chuckling to himself. He didn't know what would be the outcome of the meeting of John and the psychiatrist, but if he knew John, it would be one the psychiatrist would never forget. Trip picked up his cell phone, typed a message, and sent a text. Things were about to get very interesting; very interesting indeed.

Chapter 13

John returned to the hallway he had just been in pacing. He finally saw an office that he knew had been vacant in the past with a sign on the door, it read Dr. Stephen Freeman. John knocked and opened the door once he heard someone call out, "come in."

John entered the room. Dr. Freeman must have just literally moved in, because there was little of nothing, as his father used to say, in the room. There was a desk on one side, a couple of chairs, and the rest of the office was filled with boxes. John glanced quickly at the ceiling. He scanned all four corners of the room and noticed one tile was slightly off in the far back corner. John smiled and looked toward the front of the room where the desk was. The man behind the desk stood and walked over to John, extending his hand. John shook the gentleman's hand.

"John, John Fowler"

"Mr. Fowler, I'm Dr. Stephen Freeman," replied the older gentleman.

"Doctor Freeman, please call me John; Mr. Fowler is my father," replied John.

"Then please call me Stephen. I don't like Steve, just Stephen," Dr. Freeman said.

"Ok good to meet you Stephen," John said. "So you need to determine if I'm nuts or fit for duty, is that about right?" Stephen was a little taken aback by John's directness. "While I'm at it, anything I say here, is it confidential?"

Stephen offered John a seat and took the other one. Stephen smiled. John thought to himself that Stephen would be a great interrogator; he made John feel so at ease. Stephen took a note pad and looked at John.

"John, I don't think you're nuts," Stephen said. "Might you have some emotions that affect you and your abilities? Yes. Might you need someone to talk to so you can work though everything? Yes." John liked Stephen. There was something about him. Maybe it was just that the man had been professionally taught how to talk to someone. John didn't know what it was, but he liked him. There was a small part of John that wondered though. It was very convenient that Stephen had been sent here. The timing of it felt odd and suspicious. There was a small part of John that thought John was very paranoid and maybe he did need one of those coats in which he could hug himself. John tried to calm himself. He didn't get to be a top notch investigator by ignoring his inner warnings, but sometimes a tree was just a tree, and not a ninja dressed up in a tree suit.

John shook his head and looked over at Stephen, who had a large grin on his face. Stephen spoke.

My guess is you're wondering about how I came here so fast." John felt his face turn a little red. Wow. This guy was good. Stephen chuckled.

"I believe you met the man behind my transfer yesterday." John was trying to piece together where he would have met the man Stephen was referring to. "I believe you had a special meeting with the President of the United States yesterday under the White House after the First Lady and David George were arrested?"

John did a mental "duh!" After the altercation had ended yesterday, a man from Quantico had led John and Trip to an area beneath the White House where the three had met with the President. It was there the man from Quantico had told John there would be no resistance from those in Quantico should he decide to return to the FBI. John looked at Stephen quizzically.

"The President requested the FBI do all they could to assist you. Well, soon to be ex-President," Stephen said. John nodded. The President was preparing to step down after the events that had transpired yesterday. He was concerned that the American people might believe he was bought by his father-in-law, Archibald Staples. Stephen continued.

"My job, John, is not to hinder you or even to keep you from being re-instated. I am simply here for you to have someone to talk to. The bureau has thought for a while they might need someone with my skills here in the New York office. Simply put, we need to meet every so often, but mostly when you need me."

John nodded. He noticed that Stephen had skipped the confidentiality part. John leaned forward in his chair, tapped his fingers together, and looked sideways at Stephen. Stephen sighed and then chuckled.

"You don't miss a thing do you?" asked Stephen. He tapped a pencil against his lip, thinking. "How's this? If you have actual concrete proof of something that is going to happen, and reveal it to me but don't report it to Trip . . . then we have a problem."

John nodded and was silent for a minute. Stephen watched John. Stephen crossed his legs and tapped the pencil against his lip. He waited on John for a few minutes. Stephen continued.

"Of course, if it's just thoughts or theories that are bouncing around in your head and you think your judgment of those things is being clouded by past events of your life, we can always talk about that in confidence." John, still leaning forward, turned his head toward Stephen and smiled a sly smile.

"Hope you're ready to listen, Stephen," John said.

Chapter 14

John sat back in the chair. He really wanted to talk this through, but he needed to get moving. It was approaching 24 hours since the senator had been kidnapped. He had to get moving on the case.

"Stephen, can you clear me so I can get going and I'll set an appointment to see you ASAP?" John asked.

"Nope," replied Stephen.

"Stephen, I'm working on a kidnapping case and every minute that passes is critical," John said.

"Then you best get to talking," replied Stephen. "Now, tell me what's been going on in your life."

John smiled. "Okay, Stephen," he thought. "If that's what you want then that's what you'll get."

"A little under twenty-four hours ago, me, my team, Trip, and the senator uncovered a cover-up by the first lady of the United States of America. We also discovered that a young man, who had watched his sister killed because of the first lady's actions, and was nearly killed as well, was plotting to take revenge on her. Trip, the senator, and I arrived in Washington. I just learned that minutes after our arrival, the senator was kidnapped. While that was going on, I hijacked a TV camera, went into the Oval Office, and recorded the first lady's confession. Afterwards, Trip arrested her and David George. I then met with your friend and the President, flew back to Washington, was offered my job back and my wife's case, both of which I declined at the time. I asked one of my team, Jessica Hammerstein, to join me at an AA meeting that night. Jessica and I have been dealing with our feelings for each other, but in the past three years she has been doing the things I should have been doing, such as contacting my friends and family, and apologizing for my actions as an alcoholic. I digress from the story.

"I spoke at the AA meeting last night for the first time after attending at least 100 over the last three years. I then went on my first date since my wife died. Jessica and I talked until 2 am or so and then we each went to our separate apartments. I got up this morning and went to my office where I was served. My in-laws are suing me for my wife's trust that was left to her by her grandparents. Apparently, there is a lot of money in that trust. I really have no idea how much. As I sat down to process all of that, my cell rang telling me that Senator Cosby had been kidnapped."

John reached over to the table between them. There were some bottled waters in an ice chest. He got one and took a drink. Stephen watched him with a bemused smile. He waited until John swallowed and then asked his question.

"Is that a typical day for you, John?"

If John had any water in his mouth he would have spewed it everywhere. John roared with laughter. He laughed for several minutes and Stephen chuckled.

"No, it's not a typical day," John replied. "My life was an abysmal mess for the last three years!" John scoffed. "Life! That's a hoot. I honestly hadn't lived for the past three years! Do you know how many seedy pictures I've taken of seedy people in seedy places? It's a miracle I can eat. Some of the things I saw were just stomach turning!" Stephen was jotting something in his notes. He stood up and walked around to his desk. Stephen signed a piece of paper. Stephen walked back to his chair and sat down. He handed the paper to John. It was his reinstatement.

"That's it?" John asked incredulously.

"You've got problems, John. Heck, we've all got problems. I have my orders, but I have my conscience as well. You said it yourself. You've lived more in the past few days than you have the past few years. I feel that taking you away from the FBI would do you more harm than good. Welcome back, John. Welcome back to the FBI, but more importantly, welcome back to life."

Tears filled John's eyes. He didn't know until that moment how much the FBI meant to him. He was back! He was finally back!

Chapter 15

John was as happy as he could remember being. As great a feeling as this was, he was very conflicted. He knew he had to continue to talk to Stephen. He had to work out the problems in his head, and he couldn't go to Trip with his concerns; not until he had everything he needed.

"Stephen, this is going to sound odd, but I need a favor," John said.

"I'll do my best to help," Stephen replied.

"I need to talk about some things." John stood up and started to pace. "There are things that don't make sense, but I can't decide if it's because something is really going on, or if it's because I've got some pent up thingamajig."

"I'm not sure thingamajig is a scientific term," began Stephen. "But we can talk a while and see if we can straighten out whatever is bothering you. Go ahead."

John started to pace and then pinch his bottom lip together while he was doing it. Stephen watched in fascination. He had heard John was a master of deduction, and to watch him in action was something. John began.

"The way I was brought back to the FBI doesn't make a lot of sense to me," John paused his pacing and looked directly at Stephen. "It doesn't make sense mostly because of what I know that a lot of people don't know. It's about how I left the FBI." John stopped talking, waiting for Stephen to sort through what he said. Stephen nodded for John to continue. John began to pace and talk.

"Everyone thinks we busted an entire crime family three years ago, but that's not entirely true. We busted everyone we had something on, but there was one member that we didn't get." John stopped, and stood still, barely breathing. Stephen found himself holding his breath.

"Who was it?" Stephen asked.

"You know him today as the alleged head of the Lucciano crime family, Robert Mariotti Jr., but back then he was simply 'The Duck'," John said. Stephen tried to look serious. Then he began to snicker. The snickers turned into full fledge laughter.

"The Duck?" Stephen asked. "The Duck?" Stephen began to shake with laughter. John smiled and waited for Stephen to ask him something. Stephen signaled for John to continue. John waited for Stephen's laughter to subside. The internal alarm was starting to go off in the back of John's head.

"I know, trust me, I know it's the craziest name ever given," John said. "No one calls him that today, but what no one realizes is Duck left the crime family about a week before we began our undercover sting. That was right about the time it became known in my team that I was to go undercover. It always bothered me a little about the timing of the whole thing. After my wife died, I didn't care if the mob put a hit out on me or not. Looking back, I do find it awful strange that it never happened."

John stopped. He didn't know if he could tell Stephen the next part. He was at a point he could say it was all crazy coincidence and conspiracy theory on his part. John knew himself well. Once he voiced the questions he had, he wouldn't let them go until he knew the answers. Stephen quietly asked a question.

"John, do you think this man had something to do with your wife's death? Did he either kill her or place a hit on her?"

"No," John replied. Emotions washed over John. "No. Oh, man." John sat down in the chair. Tears were coming to his eyes. He had sworn to himself this was over.

"Let it out, John," Stephen said.

"I've been letting out tears for three years, Stephen."

"That's right, John, but let the words out, express your feelings. Tell me what you're holding on to that you haven't told apparently anyone. "

John looked down at the floor. "I think my wife was murdered and I don't think it had anything to do with me. I'm supposed to be this great detective and I can't figure out who or why my wife was killed. Don't you see, if it had something to do with me, I could punish myself. I could pay for my sins. I could drink myself to death and not regret it for one minute, but it's not my fault." John was freely sobbing. "Stephen, I think she was killed . . . just because."

Stephen nodded. "And the explosion?"

John waved his hand in the air like he was annoyed with the rank amateur question. "A cover-up; fire is one of the greatest weapons in covering something up. If done right . . . " John left his thought hanging. John slammed both of his fists against the arms of the chair. Stephen smiled a sad smile and nodded.

"Why couldn't it be my fault, Stephen? Why? I could punish me, I could. I can't catch whoever did this and until I do . . . I can't move on. It's not fair. I'm alive and she's dead. It's not fair she's dead, but she is. She's dead, and I'm the one that should be," John sat there, head down. He looked at Stephen. "I thought I was past this."

"John, you're not past it, until you're past it. What can I say, you've got a form of survivor's guilt; you know, a thingamajig." John laughed. He dried the tears on his face. Stephen studied John for a minute and then spoke. "You weren't done with your concerns were you?"

John glanced at Stephen sideways as he drank some water. John liked Stephen, and wanted to consider him a friend, but John was afraid that wasn't possible. John sat the bottle down. "I've gotta say, Stephen," John began. "You're good."

Chapter 16

"So I'm guessing you've read my file?" John asked. Stephen nodded. "Then I think there might be a little something in there about me being interrogated by 'The Hammer' and how well that went?" Stephen winced. "What it didn't tell was how I blessed out reporters, my in-laws, parents, and anyone I felt like after the funeral. Jessica covered for me on all of those occasions. She even, according to her, began dating my buddy to find out about me."

John was up and walking again. "What really bothers me is they both gave a slightly different story of what happened. They both claim they asked the other out. Not a big deal, but it's one of many small strange things." John stopped. "If I sound crazy, you'll tell me, right?"

"John," Stephen began. "You do sound a little like a conspiracy theorist, but that doesn't mean you're wrong."

John continued with the story and pacing.

"The next inconsistency we have is the supposed DVD or some type of recording done by David George. Chet claimed he saw a video, and there isn't one in evidence. I also asked David George about it. Now I admit, David's not the greatest witness in the world, but I believe him." Stephen looked at John skeptically. "I asked him, if he was the one who killed those four people would he have taped it. He replied that wouldn't be a very smart thing to do." Stephen nodded that he understood and motioned for John to continue.

"The last thing that concerns me is something that I dismissed at the time but now that I've had a little time to think about it, really bothers me. According to Trip and the Senator, Arthur is the one who demanded me back in the FBI." John stopped walking and looked at Stephen. Stephen looked absolutely perplexed.

"Let me be frank here, John," Stephen said. "Doesn't Arthur hate your guts?"

"Exactly!" John exclaimed. "Why would Arthur want me? I messed up and asked the Senator and Trip if that is what happened. Now it may have been what they wanted, but how do I know someone didn't encourage Arthur to do it. I can make loose connections to one person in every one of these scenarios except the one involving Duck, and I haven't looked into that one." Stephen looked very confused. While John had been talking alarms were going off in his head. John was 90% certain he knew what was going on in the FBI.

"Archibald Staples," John said. Stephen looked at John like he was mentally sizing John for a straightjacket.

"Arthur, the Senator, and Archibald come from the same circle," John began.

"So that's how you tie Arthur into wanting you back?" Stephen asked.

"Right, now if there is a mole," John began. "Which I have to wonder with the Duck thing, did Archibald use the mole to get me to come back to the FBI to protect his daughter's life?" Stephen looked at John sharply.

"Okay, let's say for a minute you're right about this," Stephen began. "How do you explain the inconsistency in Jessica and Chet dating?"

"One of them was trying to keep tabs on me and finding out what the other knew about me. My guess is they were trying to find out if I had connected Archibald to the Duck. From the best I can tell they broke up about the time the original quadruple homicide happened. If Jason Sparks; the first person allegedly murdered by David George in Afghanistan, if his murder was in the paper, then Archibald probably sent one of his men to the funeral. He may have hid from some distance away from the service and taped it. He then either showed it to Chet, if Chet was the mole, or made sure Chet knew where to see it on the internet if someone else was the mole." John paused for a second. "You can do that on the internet, right?" Stephen nodded. He sat for a second thinking, tapping the pencil against his lip and nodding his head.

"So Archibald, knowing the Senator from days gone by and knowing Arthur knew of your reputation, figured the one person who could figure everything out, save his daughter, and give him time to assemble a world class law team was you? You realize that's very thin?" Stephen asked. John nodded.

Stephen leaned back in his chair. "Of course if Archibald is the lynchpin behind all of this, it doesn't have to make sense," Stephen said. John smiled at Stephen. Stephen was nodding. "We both know that the people who do these things tend to do things that make sense to them. What we think of as making sense really doesn't apply. So then why was the Senator kidnapped?"

John grimaced, "I'm glad you said that part about making sense to me and you, because I could be going out on a limb on this one." Stephen raised his eyebrows. John looked a little sheepish.

"This ought to be good," Stephen said.

Chapter 17

"Stay with me," John said. "Luke is in love with the first lady. That seems to be confirmed by every member of the Secret Service. I know he met with the Senator the night before last. Luke says he was trying to get Bruce on the case because Archibald said Bruce understood that type of society and the secrets they held."

Stephen gaffed. "Bruce Cosby is one of the most incompetent agents around!"

John smiled, he really liked Stephen. "My guess is he was trying to get Bruce on the case but when that didn't work he planned to kidnap the Senator. He wanted to use the kidnapping as leverage to get Bruce to offer to take the case." Stephen looked confused again. "Sorry, I forget you weren't there, Bruce turned down the case because he thought it was too cold and it could never be solved."

"Okay, John, I can buy all of that, but why?" Stephen asked. "Isn't that going against what Archibald had in mind? He got you on the case to start with and now he's helping Luke?"

"I admit this is where I think it's very, very thin," John replied. "My gut says this idiot was so in love with Lisa he called Archibald and told him his crazy plan. We've seen men become infatuated with women before and do things that you or I would not call normal."

Stephen was nodding and playing back John's last statement in his head. "So you think Luke took his infatuation to the next level." John nodded, and he continued his explanation.

"Now remember, the Senator has tried for years to nail Archibald. How many hearings have there been involving Archibald Industries?" Stephen thought for a moment.

"More than I care to count," Stephen replied. "So basically, you think Archibald went along with the plan to mess with the Senator and it got away from him?" John nodded grimly. Stephen shook his head. "Wow. Sadly, that would all work." Stephen looked at John with a quizzical look. "You mentioned Bruce earlier, how does he fit in, John?"

"I was getting to that," John replied. "Bruce didn't put down in the file the Senator has been missing since last night. Not only that, he never told anyone! We all thought this case was a few hours old." Stephen about dropped his pencil in disbelief. That changed this case from being a few hours old to almost a day old. Everyone has heard the saying the first 48 hours are the most important. For Bruce to not report that detail . . . Stephen was stunned. John continued. "You know it could be grief."

"It could," Stephen said. "Or it could be blackmail! John, you have to report this and the part about Chet. If Chet is fabricating, or even worse, destroying evidence, Trip needs to know." Stephen was very firm. John felt a knot in his stomach. John was 100% convinced internally now, he just needed proof.

"I already have reported Bruce; as for Chet, I have no proof." John looked at Stephen directly in the eye and spoke his next statement very softly. "I'm worried that the man I wanted to call my friend is not who I thought he was." Stephen begrudgingly nodded. John looked tired. It had been a trying couple of days. It was times like this he hated his deduction skills. John waited for Stephen. Stephen spoke softly.

"What's your plan, John?"

"I'm going to see if I can pair up with Bruce. I'm going to use the excuse that I'm going to keep an eye on him and make sure he doesn't snap or do something foolish. I'm going to have both Chet and Bruce's IT guys do a check on phone calls to Archibald, and I'm going to go talk to the one person that knows the Senator and his archenemy, Archibald, better than anyone."

Stephen stood up and walked over to John. He looked John right in the eye.

"Are you ready to face Arthur, John?" Stephen asked.

"No, but I have to and I have the one thing that I know will make him talk." Stephen raised an eyebrow questioningly. "I have the information he wants on his daughter's death. I can also promise him when this is over I will do everything in my power to bring that person to justice."

Stephen nodded. John turned to leave. As he reached the door Stephen asked him one final question.

"John, what is justice in your book?"

"Let's pretend you didn't ask me that question," John replied. "If I tell you the answer to that you'll take away my reinstatement." John opened the door and walked out. As the door closed, Stephen sat down his pad and pulled out a cell phone. He typed out a text, and paused for a second. He didn't want to send the message but he knew what would happen if he didn't. Stephen sighed and hit send.

Jessica Hammerstein
New York FBI Office

Chapter 18

Jessica sat in her office, deep in the foxhole. Past all of Chet's computer equipment, there were three offices. The offices all had glass windows looking out into the foxhole, with blinds that could be drawn. Jessica had drawn the blinds and had shut the door so she could work on paperwork.

Jessica stretched in her chair. She had been working on what she thought would be simple paperwork. She should have known that anything involving the first lady and kidnapping would be anything but simple. Her mind kept returning to what John had asked her about a recording of the quadruple homicide.

She had known John for a long, long time, and she knew John didn't make mistakes like that. John could have been three sheets to the wind, but if he said someone had mentioned a recording, then someone had mentioned a recording.

Jessica thought back to the beginning of the last case when the three of them had met in John's private investigator office. John had quickly seen that Chet's and Jessica's story of who asked who out had inconsistencies. This didn't sit well with Jessica at all. If John started digging, then everything could come out; Jessica didn't think John would understand. He wasn't there those three years and didn't understand what had happened. A sick worry started in Jessica's stomach. There was a knock on her door. She looked up and saw John.

"Jess, can you get a team together to tail Luke?" John asked.

Jessica looked at John, puzzled.

"I'm pretty sure Luke has something to do with this. He's about to be released and we need to follow his every move. I've gotta run. I'll be back in a few."

With that John was gone. Jessica started to pick up the phone, but the cold worry came into her stomach. She knew what she had to do. She pulled out her cell phone. She swore she would never do this again, but she had to let him know. He was the only person that could stop John from uncovering the truth. Jessica typed in a message and paused. She knew once she sent this message there was no turning back. Jessica hit send and exhaled. It was done. Jessica prayed she could live with the consequences.

Chet Morris
Foxhole

Chapter 19

Chet, with his headphones on, sat in front of the huge monitors, working. He waved at John as he walked by. Chet kept an eye on a little traffic light that was on the bottom left corner of one of his menu bars. When the traffic light turned green, Chet hit a few buttons and an image came on the screen.

The screens faced away from the offices in the foxhole so even if Jessica had her blinds open, she couldn't see what Chet was working on. Chet also had a kill switch he had programmed that would automatically remove the images he was watching on the monitors in front of him if he were to flip the switch. He hated to have to be this secretive, but he had his orders and if he didn't follow them . . . well, Chet didn't want to think about that.

In front of him was a recording of John and Stephen. The recording on the computer had been made from the camera Chet had planted in Stephen's office before Stephen moved in this morning. Chet had no worry about anyone seeing anything. He had installed motion detectors in the hallway that would cause this program to close and another innocent program to pop-up if anyone came within fifty feet of the foxhole.

Chet listened as John told Stephen his suspicions about Luke, and then his fears about Chet. Chet shook his head. He was afraid this would happen. He thought back to the meeting he and John had in John's living room when Chet was first trying to recruit John back into the FBI a few days ago. Chet's orders were simple that day. Get John Fowler on the quadruple homicide case; any means necessary. Chet had done exactly what he had been asked to do, but now it was coming back to bite him. John could sniff out lies and inconsistencies anywhere. He would dig at them like a dog digging apart a yard looking for a bone. If John couldn't figure out what was bothering him about a case, then he would get Jessica to take you into the box. By the time Jessica was done with you, a person would admit to every crime they had ever committed.

Chet knew he had made a mistake when he first talked to John. Chet had told John too much about Chet's relationship with Jessica. Chet pulled up his online poker account and stared at it. The balance read $0.00. Chet shook his head disgustedly and pulled out his cell phone. He typed a message and paused. Chet looked back at the account and spoke softly to himself.

"If you do the crime, you gotta do the time."

Chet hit send. He took a deep breath and went to work. Chet opened up a dummy email account he had made. He typed in an address and sent a copy of the video he had been watching. He then erased all proof he had been to the poker site and the camera feed. He then erased all traces of what he had been doing and shut down the computer. Only someone who knew exactly what they were looking for and was a world class computer hacker had a chance to find a trace of what he had done. Chet walked out of the foxhole. He needed some air.

Jeremiah Cosby
At an Undisclosed Location

Chapter 20

Jeremiah knew only two things. One he had a bag over his head, and two, he had to go to the bathroom really, really bad. He had no idea how much time had passed since he had been taken yesterday, well he assumed it was yesterday he was taken. All he could remember was talking to Luke and then nothing. He had awoken in what he thought was a van. He was bound and already had the bag over his head. Jeremiah snapped back to the present. He was going to go to the bathroom, the question was where.

"Look here, now," Jeremiah began. "I understand I'ma at your mercy, but you have to let a gentleman go to the bathroom."

Jeremiah listened and heard nothing. He then heard a door open. Jeremiah heard footsteps cross the room and felt his hands unshackled. He was led across the room. He heard a door open, a flick of a switch, was pushed in the room, and finally felt the binding around the bag removed. The door was shut behind him. He heard someone yell through the door to, "holler when you're done." Jeremiah took off the bag and looked around. It was a simple bathroom with no window, or mirror. Jeremiah took care of business, and tried to wash his face. He couldn't tell if he got it clean or not without a mirror. He put the bag back over his head and then hollered out. He heard footsteps and the door open. A chuckle came from in front on him. He felt the bag get ripped from his face and his heart sank. If he was able to identify his kidnappers, he knew his life wouldn't be worth much. Jeremiah kept his eyes closed.

"What's the matter, old man?" The voice in front of him asked. "Afraid of not seeing tomorrow? Open your eyes!" Jeremiah opened his eyes and gave a sigh of relief. The man in front of him was wearing a presidential Halloween mask.

"You already know our boss. You know the Secret Service guy, Luke? I just want to make sure you don't know me." Jeremiah opened his mouth in astonishment and started to speak. He couldn't however because the kidnapper in front of him hit him with a stun gun and Jeremiah was knocked out. The kidnapper dragged Jeremiah back to his chair. He then shackled and bagged Jeremiah. The man walked out of the room, closed the door, and made a phone call.

"Boss, I did it. He thinks that Luke is in charge of the kidnapping," said the kidnapper.

Archibald Staples
Virginia

Chapter 21

"Good," Archibald said into his cell phone. "Stay there until you hear from me. Once Luke is released from the FBI, you leave and we'll send McDonald there." Archibald listened to something on the other end. He then hung up the phone.

Archibald stared out over his estate. It had been a busy morning. He had received a text from his mole earlier that simply read, "He suspects." Archibald knew exactly what this meant. He turned toward his bodyguard who was outside with him. Archibald walked over to the bodyguard and talked with a very low voice.

"Did you do what I asked with Duck?" Archibald asked. The bodyguard nodded. "Good, we can't be traced to Duck, his person is in place, and we've tied up the loose end of Luke. Why on Earth Veronica trusted that idiot, I have no idea. She may have had some master plan, but since I'm not privy to it, I'll just have to do what's best for me." The bodyguard smiled.

Archibald watched the lawyers still working in his office. The lawyers thought they could have Veronica out of jail by this afternoon; tomorrow afternoon at the latest. They also thought she could beat all the charges. She would lose her marriage and her political aspirations were over, but she would be safe, and most importantly so would Archibald. Archibald started to walk away and then he paused. He turned to the bodyguard and asked him a question.

"Did he do the thing?" Archibald asked. The bodyguard looked confused. "You know, 'If it looks like one and talks like one' and then shrug his shoulders?" The bodyguard grinned broadly.

"Yes, he did, sir," the bodyguard answered. "I didn't crack a smile, but I really wanted to. Is it true, sir?" Archibald looked at the bodyguard questioningly. "You know, that the last guy that called him the Duck to his face he choked to death?" Archibald shrugged his shoulders.

"Who knows," Archibald replied. "According to the story no one has ever found the body to find out how he died." The bodyguard laughed as Archibald headed back inside.

Trip
New York FBI Headquarters

Chapter 22

Trip was in a tough spot. He had just received two texts and both were disturbing. John had a plan, but what it was Trip didn't know. Trip sighed, and turned and looked out the window. He wondered why he even bothered some days. He thought life would have been less complicated with John gone, but he found out the hard way that was not true. John's team had been through so much when John left that Trip did what he had never done . . . he stuck his neck out. It was against everything inside of Trip to do that. Trip was BY THE BOOK. It was just that simple. There was nothing Trip could imagine that would change him. . . until Sam.

What John didn't know was that time had all but stood still since the day Sam died over three years ago for Chet, Jessica, and himself. Trip knew there was going to be a day of reckoning. He had known that the day the three of them decided that John had to come back.

The biggest secret they held from John was possibly the most damaging. What John didn't know was that Sam had come to Trip, Chet, and Jessica before her death. She suspected someone was following her. She wasn't worried about herself as much as she was concerned John had been made and she was being followed to see if John's next move could be determined. She didn't have concrete proof. Trip thought she was being paranoid due to all the drinking John had been doing and the hours he kept undercover. Still, Trip couldn't chance that she was right and had some friends in the NYPD. After a few phone calls Trip had someone watching out for John. John knew nothing about this. As for Sam, Trip never offered protection in any way. Trip felt himself start to tremble.

Trip set his jaw and tried to hold his emotions in check. A single tear fell down his cheek. Trip blamed himself for Sam's death. Chet told Trip it was his fault for not watching out for his best friend's wife. Jessica said it was her fault for not watching out better for her best friend. As guilty as they each thought they were, none of them held a candle to the internal grief that John held inside. For three years, when they weren't secretly watching John to make sure he didn't self-destruct, the three of them followed every lead on the Sam Fowler case and they each came up with nothing. They all said the same thing; the only person who could solve this case was John. It was during this case that Trip learned something that should have made him immediately dismiss one of his agents, but he didn't. He did something he never did; he covered for them.

John was right about the Mafia case; there had been a mole. It wasn't like John thought, but there was one just the same. When John found out, and Trip knew it was a matter of when, and not if, John could have them all fired. There wouldn't be a thing the three of them could say in their defense, and they all knew it.

Chapter 23

A knock on the door brought Trip back to reality. Trip turned and saw John. John looked a little concerned. Trip, fearing his voice might crack from the emotion he was trying to hold in check inside, waved John in.

"Trip," John began. "Are you okay?"

Trip waved John off.

John continued, "Look, I know I'm not the poster boy of how to deal with things, but talking does help sometimes, and I don't mean me. There are people who you can talk to that might help."

Trip looked perturbed. "So let me get this straight, one meeting with the good doctor downstairs and you think everyone who's having a bad day needs to see a shrink?"

John nodded slowly, his lips pressed together. He had obviously broached a sensitive subject. Wheels began to turn in John's head. He had never seen Trip like this. Trip kept his emotions in check better than anyone. There were several explanations for Trip's reaction. The most plausible reason being all they had been through the past few days stirred up emotions inside of Trip that he wasn't use to dealing with. It was the other explanations running through John's head that worried him. John knew he needed to proceed carefully.

Look, Trip," John said. "It was just a suggestion. And since I've obviously overstepped my bounds I'm gonna keep going. If you see someone, see someone outside of the FBI."

Trip looked at John sharply. "Let me guess, the good doctor didn't reinstate you and now you don't like him?"

"Wrong," said John as he laid the reinstatement papers on Trip's desk. "I just don't think everything needs to be handled in-house. Take it from me, this job can make you do things you never thought you would." John had a rue smile on his face as he spoke.

Trip barked a laugh and examined the paperwork. He opened John's file and placed it inside. Trip pulled out John's new shield and ID and handed it to John. John placed it in his suit pocket, right back where it belonged. Trip leaned back in his chair. He looked at John and tried to decide the best way to proceed.

"What's your next step?" Trip asked.

"Well," John began. "I want to team with Bruce." Trip looked stunned. "Hear me out, there are two reasons Bruce didn't tell us about the timeline. One he's in on the kidnapping, two he actually cares about his dad and this has affected him. Either way, by keeping him close to me I can figure out the majority of his moves and keep him from doing something stupid." Trip nodded. He picked up a piece of paper.

"This gives me the authority to let Bruce on the case," Trip said nodding toward the paper.

"In my opinion, sir," John said. "That is exactly what we need to do. We also need to do a couple of other things, I need Chet to work on tracking down any electronic leads on Luke, and I'd like Bruce's IT guy to do the same thing."

Trip sat up very straight in his chair. He really didn't like where this was going.

"I'm not done yet," John said. He knew how things sounded, but he had no choice in what he was doing. "I want Jessica and a member of Bruce's team to go over the findings of both Chet and Bruce's IT guys together. I want Jessica and a member of Bruce's team to go over any paper trail together. Trip, it's real simple. I want two sets of eyes, one from my team and one from Bruce's team, on each piece of evidence."

Chapter 24

Trip was on the verge of being furious. John had Trip believing that John didn't trust his two teammates. John smiled inwardly. Trip had Jessica's and Chet's back. John had to make sure of that. John knew he was playing a dangerous game, but it was necessary. John had a serious hunch on several things at the moment. The first was Luke had something to do with the Senator's kidnapping. The second, there was a mole in the FBI. The third, and the most troubling, was one of the three people John had any chance of calling friends, was in deep trouble. John thought he could solve the third problem, but he had to test out one small thing before he could be sure.

"Trip," John said fiercely. "This isn't the time to sugarcoat things. We have a senator that has been missing for 24 hours. I need as many eyes on this as possible to make sure we don't miss anything."

Trip's mind was whirling. Trip slowly looked up at John, nodding. Trip was slapping his head mentally. Did John just bait him to see how he'd react? Blast that man! He'd only been active, well, minutes officially, and it was like he had never missed a beat. Trip knew he had to calm down and agree to this. He didn't need John digging into what happened while he was gone.

You're absolutely right, John," Trip replied. "I'll get everyone started. What about you?"

John sighed. "I've already got Jessica setting up a tail on Luke. I wanted to clear the partner thing with you before I went forward with my main plan. I'm going to go talk to Chet and Jessica real quick and then Bruce and I are going to go talk to someone who knows the Staples the best." Trip had been dialing the phone, but with that statement by John he slowly hung it up and looked at John. Trip swallowed, afraid to ask if the person John was going to talk to was who Trip thought it was. John turned and walked to the door. He stopped, turned back toward Trip, and spoke.

"I'm going to see my in-laws." With that, John walked out of Trip's office. Trip sat still for a second. He then began to lightly chuckle. The chuckle broke out into a roaring laugh. What he wouldn't give to be a fly on the wall and hear the conversation that would take place between John and the Moores.

Chapter 25

John knocked on Jessica's door. Chet was nowhere to be seen in the Foxhole. He heard Jessica yell to enter so he opened the door. Jessica smiled when she saw him.

"Hey, Jess," John began. "I was wondering if you had a few minutes." Jess offered him a seat and John sat. "I know I've been gone a while, but . . . well, do I have to use my office over here, or can I use the desk over by Chet? You know I like to work out in the open."

Jessica smiled. "John, you can work anywhere you want. I usually work out there as well. It's just when I'm dealing with this paperwork, I can't handle of all Chet's flashing screens. Is this what you wanted to talk to me about?"

John shifted in his seat. "Jess, the senator has been missing for almost 24 hours." Jess dropped her pencil. "I need you and one of Bruce's men to go over everything Chet and Bruce's IT guy does. I want two eyes on everything to make sure we haven't missed anything."

Jessica tapped her pen on the table. She looked at John hard. "You want me to go over Chet's findings?"

John shook his head no very slowly. Jessica's nostrils flared. She started to speak, but John cut her off.

"Jess, Bruce is the person Luke told that the senator has been missing since yesterday . . . I don't know what's going on, but I haven't got time to babysit. I need everyone crosschecking each other. That way even if something shady is going on this may deter anyone from messing with evidence in any way."

Jessica tapped her pen on the table again. John knew she wasn't happy. She nodded.

"John, I don't like it, but you're right," Jessica said.

"Mind if we change the subject for a minute? There is something I've wanted to ask you," John asked. Jessica beamed and leaned across the desk. "The way you danced the other night . . . being an FBI agent wasn't your first choice, was it?"

Jessica smiled and leaned back in her chair.

"No," she replied simply. "No, I went to a dance school. I paid my own way. My parents weren't too happy with me. I was there two years when I hurt my knee. It wasn't anything that would bother me in everyday life, or even anything that would stop me from passing an FBI physical, but it was enough that would limit me in dancing for a couple of years. The school was very cutthroat, and I had to be at 100%. So I took some time off from dancing."

Jessica paused in the story. John was hanging on every word. She had never known someone to naturally be this interested in a person's background. In her experience the only time someone was as interested as this; it was either a first date, or she was being interrogated. She decided to see where this led and continued.

"I decided I had borrowed too much money just to quit school, so I decided to do something practical while I waited for my knee to heal. I took some classes and it led to the FBI."

John nodded. "I bet that cost a lot of money," he stated.

"It cost a fortune!" Jessica exclaimed. "It wasn't just student loans. That wouldn't cover all the costs, so I had to take out private loans as well. My parents wouldn't pay for any of it because they thought dancing wouldn't make any money. They thought that I would abandon my degree as soon as my knee had rehabbed. In case you haven't noticed, the cost of living in New York isn't exactly cheap either."

John was nodding as he listened. The private loan part really began to bug him. Student loans were controlled by the government now, but private . . . John reached a decision in his mind quickly. He realized Jessica had finished and now there was an uncomfortable pause between them.

John," Jessica began. "If there is something you want to know, please come right out and ask me and don't beat around the bush."

John studied Jessica's face very carefully. He knew she was just seconds from breaking into full interrogator mode. John didn't ever want to be there again.

"Jess, I was just curious, that's all," John stated. He got up to leave. "Look, I need to let Chet know what's going on and then Bruce and I are going on a little trip. I don't want Bruce to leave my sight. For whatever reason, something is up with him." John started to leave and paused. He knew this would get Jessica off of the attack with him. "By the way, you may want to alert the Virginia State Police and Quantico. Bruce and I are going to go talk to the Moores about Archibald." With that, he tipped his hat and headed out the door.

Jessica stared at the door for a minute. Once John got back, if he and Sam's father didn't kill each other, she was going to have a long talk with John; as John's mom use to say, "A come to Jesus meeting." She didn't think John was going to like it, but she really didn't care. There were too many things insinuated in their conversation, and if they were ever going to have any kind of relationship, then there needed to be trust. Jessica smiled to herself. She hadn't let a man get her this upset in a long time. She didn't know where things would lead with John. She spoke out loud softly.

Sam, how did you ever put up with that irritating man?" Jessica was sure Sam was somewhere laughing at her.

Chapter 26

John walked out of Jessica's office and noticed Chet hadn't come back to the Foxhole yet. John had a pretty good idea of where he was. John didn't like what he did to Jessica and he really didn't like what he was about to do to Chet. John had a good idea of what was going on, and he knew that part of this was his fault. Well, it wasn't, but John wouldn't let his team get hurt the way they had been if he had been around instead of being undercover and then leaving the FBI.

John knew he needed to fix things, and he knew what he needed to do to fix things, but he was going to have to eat many portions of humble pie to do so. John shuddered from thinking about what he would have to do and moved the thoughts from his mind. John began thinking about his conversation from earlier with Dr. Freeman about the reoccurring participant family to this case and the previous two he worked on; the Staples.

John knew Veronica was involved in the last case. He had suspicions this kidnapping had something to do with Veronica and her father, but he had always wondered about the Mafia case from years ago. Did someone tip off the Duck? If John had never heard of the Duck again, he never would have thought twice about it. The fact the man was known as the alleged head of the Lucciano crime family . . . something was rotten in Denmark. How had Robert Mariotti Jr, the man known as the Duck, managed to have no dealings with everyone the FBI targeted on John's undercover operation? Better yet, how did he manage to come back and take control of everything? The thing that bothered John the most, how does someone who was simply a loan shark, with one of the most ridiculous names in the history of the Mafia, climb the ranks that quickly? This was the part that bothered John more than anything.

John realized he had reached the roof of the FBI building while thinking. He looked around and saw his friend. Chet was sitting on some type of metal case on the roof, looking over the city. John scratched his chin. He ran things through his mind one more time and could come up with no other explanation of what had happened. This was one of those times John hated his abilities. John approached Chet.

Chapter 27

John walked up beside Chet and just stood there for a moment, silent. John gazed out over the city. He had to admit, New York was beautiful from the top of the building. Sam use to love to come to the office just to look out over the city. John smiled to himself. Sam always looked for the good in everything. It wasn't that John didn't appreciate the beauty of the city, but he was a country boy at heart. John had grown up in a small rural area in Western Kentucky, and there were times he just missed home. Sam . . . Sam just loved the city. She loved the culture, the buildings, the bustle; she just loved everything about it. John shook his head.

"Chet," John began. "You okay, buddy?"

Chet looked at John. John noticed several things instantly. Chet had dark circles under his eyes; he could see the tension in Chet's skin around his head. Chet's nails had been bitten. Frankly, Chet looked like something was eating him from the inside out; all of that took John less than a second. Chet tried to smile reassuringly, but it was to no avail, John already knew the words coming out of Chet's mouth were a lie.

"Yeah," Chet said with a wave of his hand. "Yeah, buddy, I'm good. Anything on the case?" John stuffed his hands in his pockets and blew out a long breath of air. Chet gave a half smile. He knew John enough to know there was something, but it wasn't good.

"Chet, this case is almost 24 hours old," John said. Chet chuckled and looked back out over the city. Inside, Chet was berating himself. Chet had already known that fact, but John didn't know that Chet knew. Chet knew he had to play it off. He turned back toward John shaking his head. He laughed as he spoke.

"Given the past few days, would you expect anything less, John?" Chet asked. John rocked back on his heels and shook his head no. John prepared himself for what he was about to tell his buddy.

"Chet," John began. "I know this isn't how we usually do things, but I need you and Bruce's IT guy to run the exact same things independently. We're 24 hours behind, and we need to have double eyes on everything." John waited for the explosion. It didn't come. Chet looked at John with sadness in his eyes. This was killing John.

"You think the senator is already dead, don't you, John?"

Chapter 28

John didn't say anything for a minute. There were really two reasons John was having double eyes on everything. The first was to make sure there wasn't a mole interfering in the investigation, and if there was to catch that person. The second; John had to cover himself. A senator being kidnapped was a high profile case, and this case was already going bad. If this case went wrong . . . John knew with him as lead investigator and just back in the FBI after a three year absence, his case work would be scrutinized. What John found so interesting was Jessica and Trip had assumed he was looking for inconsistencies, and possibly a mole, while Chet immediately thought the Senator was dead.

John's heart sank. There were several reasons Chet could have thought that. There was the obvious; Chet knew the Senator was dead. But that just didn't feel right to John. What felt right, was that Chet had so many personal setbacks in his life; he just drifted toward the negative. John knew blaming himself right now wasn't the answer. He put his hand on Chet's shoulder.

"I don't know, Chet," John answered honestly. "I just don't know. What I do know is that if we can find one extra clue by doing this, then that's what we need to do. Time is critical." Chet nodded and stood up. John moved his hand off of Chet's shoulder as he did.

You're right, John," Chet said. "We need every edge we can get."

"Just like poker?" John asked, smiling.

Chet cracked a big smile and nodded.

"Hey," John began. "I've always wanted to ask you something. You play poker by the math, right?" Chet nodded. "Say your opponent has pocket aces and you have the 7 and the 8 of clubs." Chet nodded. "Ok, now say the flop comes 9 of clubs, 6 of clubs, and another suit 8, what do you do?

Chet's smile nearly cracked his face. "I try to get my opponent to put in everything he has! You've got the odds in your favor. You have to make the other guy throw the better hand away, or you have two chances to make your hand, either on the turn or on the river!"

John shook his head, "But, what if it's your whole bankroll, Chet? I mean what if it's your mortgage and food money . . . I mean what if it's everything you have?"

Chet looked incredulous. "John, you do realize you're going to win almost 65% of the time, right?"

John put his hand on Chet's shoulder. "But, Chet, your behind in the hand, and that means the other 35% or so of the time, you're gonna lose."

Chet's face fell. John knew. In that minute there was no question in his mind, he knew. John looked Chet in the eye.

"How much, Chet?" Chet looked up sharply at John. John repeated himself, softly. "How much have you lost?" John took a deep breath and asked his next question even more softly. "How much do you owe?"

"I'd rather not talk about it," Chet replied. John nodded. John hated himself for what he did, but his suspicions had been confirmed. John shifted uncomfortably. Chet started to walk to the door.

"You know there are meetings for it, right?" John asked.

"I'm already going," Chet replied continuing for the door. John took a deep breath. He had to give something back to Chet.

"I spoke last night, Chet. For the first time ever, I spoke." Chet stopped in his tracks. He had already heard about what happened on the tape, but for John to share this with him . . .

"Did it help?" Chet asked, his back still turned.

"She's still dead, Chet," John replied. Chet spun and walked back to John angrily.

"John, she's not coming back, and there is a woman down there that loves you more than she knows what to do about it!" John had never seen Chet quite so passionate before. "Do not let this terrible thing that happened kill you, or your life! You deserve to live, and you deserve to have a life! The person that deserves to pay will! Do you understand me? We'll catch him, John, I promise you we'll catch him, and when we do, if you can't pull the trigger, I will!"

Chet realized what he had just done, and was scared he had gone too far. John looked Chet in the eye and smiled broadly.

"You do know you just told a federal officer you plan on shooting a man, right?" Chet nodded. John smiled. "I may just hold you to that promise, sir." Chet smiled and headed back to the door.

John knew what he had to do. He sighed, turned, and looked back over New York. Chet and Jessica would get things started here. Now all John had to do was take one man who hated him, to see another man that hated John more. John pulled out his new FBI ID and looked at it.

"I know how to come back," he said out loud to no one.

Chapter 29

John headed back inside and began to look for Bruce. He looked for a few minutes before someone he had never seen in the office before told him Trip wanted to see John in Trip's office. John made a beeline for Trip's office. John opened Trip's door and immediately regretted it. Trip was sitting in his chair, looking very uncomfortable. Bruce was in the chair across from Trip. Bruce was crying with his head buried in his hands. John tried to leave, but Trip waved John in, insistently.

"John," Trip began. "Bruce and I have been talking, and it seems he forgot to tell us a few things this morning." John had never felt more uncomfortable in his life. He had no idea Bruce had the ability to cry over anyone, well, except for Bruce. Trip looked like he'd rather be anywhere on the Earth rather than where he was right now. No, scratch that. Trip looked like he'd rather be anywhere in the universe.

"John," Bruce began to talk through his sobs. "John, I'm so sorry." Bruce still had his face buried in his hands. John looked at Trip. Trip shrugged his shoulders with his hands out in the air and mouthed, "I don't know what to do." Bruce began to try to speak again.

"John, I know I screwed up." With the word "up" Bruce began to sob. John motioned to Trip to join him outside.

"Bruce," John said quickly. "We're gonna give you a second to collect yourself, and then you and I are going to go interview some people and see if we can't get a lead on your dad." Bruce nodded, hands still covering his face. John and Trip hurried outside and shut the door.

After the door closed, Bruce lowered his hands. His eyes were dancing with mischievous evil, and there was a grin about to split Bruce's head in two. Bruce began to chuckle to himself quietly.

"John, you haven't got a chance against me."

Chapter 30

John and Trip stood in the hallway outside Trip's office, both were flustered. As they stood there a second Trip started to chuckle. John hit Trip on the shoulder, and that just made things worse. Trip began to laugh out loud. John grabbed Trip by the arm and led him around the corner, away from Trip's office.

"What are you doing?" John asked.

"Oh, for the love of Pete, John!" Trip exclaimed. "That guy hasn't shown one ounce of anything for anyone in all the years I've known him except for himself. After all the grief he gave you, you're defending him?"

John looked Trip dead in the eye.

"Yeah, Trip, because I know what losing someone when you're only wrapped up in yourself does to you."

Trip stopped laughing immediately. He became very silent, and obviously a little embarrassed.

"Don't get me wrong, Trip," John continued. "That guy is a jerk, but he obviously has some feelings for his father."

"Is that one of the famous John reads telling you that?" Trip snapped. Trip regretted what he said as soon as he said it. John was right; no one deserved to be mocked when they had lost someone. Trip was still irritated by being called out on it by John. Trip started to apologize but John waved it off.

"It's fine, Trip," John said. "Actually, I'll let you in on a little secret. Bruce is one of the few people I can't get a read on. It's funny actually, Sam used to say she felt like every time Bruce looked at her, there was a hate in him that just sent shivers up her spine. I always tried to see it, but never could. I really think it was just Sam being upset at how much Jeremiah seemed to care about her and he really had nothing to do with Bruce."

"I thought the only people you really couldn't get a read on were sociopaths?" Trip asked.

"Well, yeah," John began. "Since they basically have nothing that tells them the difference inside about right and wrong, you can't decipher their expressions, or some subtle tell from their body. It's not that there aren't tells, it's just that they don't tell a consistent story. You might find physical evidence on them, but you can't make any connection with their body language."

"Maybe Bruce is a sociopath," Trip stated. John looked shocked.

"Trip, you need to knock it off!" John exclaimed. "You know full well the evaluations we all go through would have caught that."

"And we all know no one would have fixed things for Bruce if they thought we might get a little something from the Senator, right?"

John groaned inwardly. Bruce had been given so many special considerations and job advancements over the years because of who he was and who his father was. The senator had never asked for any of it; in fact, what promotions Bruce had received sickened the senator. John and Trip had learned over the years that those in power believed that the senator would favor the FBI with little perks just because of the station his son held. John wished he could tell them how far off base they were with that line of thinking.

"Trip, I'm going to get Bruce and go take care of this case. He did get permission to work it, right?" Trip nodded. John took off, shaking his head. Trip stood in the hallway listening to John tell Bruce to come with him. Trip tried to get the thought he had out of his mind. What he was thinking couldn't be possible. Trip shook his head and watched John leave, but kept having the same thought, what if it was possible?

Chapter 31

John and Bruce sat on the helicopter that was flying them to Virginia. John felt very uncomfortable. He didn't know what to say to Bruce. John still couldn't believe what Trip had said earlier about Bruce. John knew better than anyone that Bruce was a jerk, but John also knew about personal loss destroying a person. Bruce kept staring at his hands.

"John," Bruce began. "Have you ever felt the life slip out of someone you were holding in your hands?"

John was more than a little bothered by that question. John knew Bruce had lost his mother at a young age. He really wasn't sure what to say.

"Well, I did have a suspect once bleed out on me, and I watched a good man die and couldn't do anything about it," John offered.

Bruce just kept looking at his hands. John was more than a little creeped out by the conversation.

"I held her, John," Bruce began. "I held her and felt the life drain from her. The feeling John . . . the feeling is incredible, and horrible, all at the same time. She looked me in the eyes as she left this world. She tried to speak John . . . she tried." John didn't know how to react. If this was how his mother died, this could explain many things about Bruce.

"I always wondered what she was trying to say," Bruce continued. "Was it important? Was she trying to get me to pass a message to someone?" Bruce looked John in the eyes. "It was the strangest feeling, John. I was the last person she saw as she slipped away. To hold someone in your hands as they died . . ."

John put his hand on Bruce's shoulder. He somewhat expected Bruce to flinch, but Bruce stayed still just staring into John's eyes.

"We'll find your father," John said softly. "We'll find him, Bruce. We'll find him alive."

"He doesn't know, John," Bruce began. "He doesn't know what I've done for him. It was just us for so long. I did so much for him, and he doesn't even know. He needs to know, John. I have to tell him."

John didn't know what to do. Bruce appeared to be in shock. John had never seen Bruce so . . . human. John just patted Bruce on the shoulder, and then squeezed it. John turned back and looked out over the countryside and wished they would land quickly. Bruce turned and looked out his window.

Bruce smiled quickly to himself. "The fool," Bruce thought. "I just told him everything. I just answered the biggest question in his life, and he thought I was talking about dear old Mom." Bruce turned back to John, the sadness back on his face.

"John, will you please keep what I talked to you about between us?" Bruce asked. "The senator doesn't need to know until I'm ready to talk to him." John gave Bruce a tight lipped smile and nodded. All John could think was how sad it was that Bruce couldn't call his own father, "Dad." All Bruce could think about was how John was just sad.

Chapter 32

Jessica knocked on Trip's door. Trip was staring out the window with his back toward the open door. He spun around in his chair when he heard the knock. He motioned Jessica in. Jessica came in and sat down. Trip got up and shut his door. He looked at Jessica, and then silently locked it. Jessica gave Trip a strange look. Trip walked around the desk, but stopped at the desk and looked out the window again. When he turned back toward Jessica, tears were in his eyes.

"Thanks for coming so quick, I know you're working on the senator's case, but . . ." Trip couldn't finish the sentence. If what he thought was true . . . Trip tried to set his jaw and get control of himself. Tears dropped from his face.

Jessica was completely stunned. She had never seen Trip like this.

"Sir . . .Trip?" She began. "What is it?"

"John said something today," Trip replied. "He said he couldn't read Bruce. We talked for a bit, and John said the only people he normally couldn't get a read on were sociopaths, and Bruce." Trip turned toward Jessica. Jessica's mind was racing with that information.

"Trip, are you suggesting . . . "Jessica couldn't finish the question.

Trip threw down Bruce's file on his desk.

"There's no psychiatric evaluation in here, and I checked in the database. "

For a minute neither said a word. Twice Jessica started to say something, but stopped. The look on Trip's face said volumes.

"Trip, are you saying . . . Trip, are you saying that Bruce is a sociopath?" Jessica finally managed to ask. Trip looked annoyed.

"A sociopath? That's it?" Trip asked. "That's what you're going with? I give you the keys to the house and you don't go past the foyer?" Trip was getting very worked up. "Jessica, John can't read him. John told me Sam was uncomfortable with Bruce."

Jessica put her hands in front of Trip to signal him to stop. This was too much too fast.

"Trip," Jessica began, choosing her words very carefully. "Before you say the words that are about to come out of your mouth, you need to think about what will happen if YOU say them. It's one thing for me or Chet or John to say this, but you are the director of this office. You can't put the genie back in the bottle. Once this is out, you'll have to suspend him. If you suspend him how can we do a proper investigation?"

Trip rubbed his palm against his head, knowing Jessica was right. For three years whoever had killed Sam had evaded the three of them. They had to move carefully.

"We can't tell John, can we?" Trip was asking this question to no one, he already knew the answer.

"No," answered Jessica. "We can't tell him until we are sure." A thought crossed Jessica's mind that she prayed wasn't true. "Trip, does John suspect?"

Trip shook his head as he answered. "No. Heck, he defended Bruce earlier when I implied he was a sociopath. And before you even ask, no I don't think Bruce is planning on killing John." Trip stared at his desk for a second. "Of course I never thought he would . . ." Trip let the sentence trail off, knowing he had to let Jessica and Chet investigate.

"Why?" Jessica simply asked. Trip looked amused.

"If he is a sociopath, does he really need a reason?" Trip walked back over to the window and stared out of it. Jessica was searching for answers in her mind but could come up with nothing.

"Is there any evidence that you know of that would link him to Sam's murder?" Jessica asked.

Trip never turned from the window. He just kept starring out the window as he shook his head no. It all fit into place for Trip. John was always getting the best of Bruce and how better for Bruce to get John back than to take away the most important thing in John's life. The worst part of all of this, if Trip was wrong, which he doubted he was, Trip could never trust Bruce again.

Chapter 33

"How would you like me to precede, sir?" Jessica asked.

Trip finally turned from the window. He looked at Jessica. She looked like Trip felt. She looked like she had been ambushed, emotionally. She looked like everything she knew in life was now wrong. If Bruce had done this . . . it meant one of their own had killed a spouse of one of theirs. Trip was sick inside.

"You're going to Quantico, and you're going to get his file," Trip answered.

"Uh, sir, you do remember Senator Cosby?" Trip grimaced. No, he had forgotten it for a moment. This couldn't get much worse. Well, now that he thought about it, it could. Trip knew who could get the file. Jessica had a slow smile crawling across her face. Everyone in the New York office knew about Thelma, but for the sake of their jobs, they pretended they didn't.

Trip took a deep breath and prepared to call Thelma. Thelma had a thing for Trip. Trip definitely did not have a thing for Thelma, at least not one he wanted to admit to anyone. Thelma worked in records at Quantico and could get anything for Trip, at a price. Trip sighed. Jessica was studying Trip. Trip rolled his eyes, sat down in his chair, and picked up the phone. He hesitated and looked at Jessica.

"For Sam," Jessica mouthed, and began to snicker.

Trip dialed the phone. The other end connected. Trip tried to take control of the phone call, but quickly failed.

"Thelma? I'm fine. Yes, it has been a while . . . uh-huh . . . uh-huh . . . I hear that's a nice place to eat . . . uh-huh . . . uh-huh . . . ." Trip looked at the ceiling. "Listen, Thelma, I need a favor." As Trip listened his eyes started to close and a look of pain crossed his face. Jessica had her

81

hand clamped over her mouth so as not to laugh out loud. Trip looked at Jessica and scowled. Jessica had to hold her hand tighter over her mouth. Trip tried to wrestle back control of the conversation.

"Thelma, I need a copy of Bruce Cosby's file. All of his evaluations, even his application to the Bureau," Trip interjected. Thelma spoke and Trip straightened in his chair, surprised. "Really . . . and why's that?" He listened for a few more seconds. "Can you get that copy?" Trip shut his eyes with the answer and shuddered. "Of course I will, Thelma; I'll be there next week." Trip looked physically pained at the next thing Thelma said. He looked at Jessica and tried to lower his voice where she couldn't see him. "You know I've got a bad back . . . " Jessica almost lost her mind with laughter. She grabbed a throw pillow from another chair and pushed it over her mouth. Trip looked very annoyed. "Okay, as soon as you can get it to me. Would you send it to my private fax?" Trip smiled with the response. "Thanks, I'll see you in a couple of weeks." Trip hung up the phone and looked very pleased with himself.

Chapter 34

Jessica lowered the pillow that had been covering her face and began to laugh loudly.

"Will you stop that?" Trip exclaimed. Jessica just continued to laugh.

"Seriously, we have important things to discuss," Trip said, mildly annoyed.

"Like your bad back?" Jessica could barely breathe she was laughing so hard.

"Oh, grow up," Trip admonished. "She wants to play laser tag." Jessica raised her eyebrows in response and her laughter intensified.

"Seriously, she wants to play laser tag. No one will play with her. I kinda feel sorry for her," Trip said. Trip's expression softened.

"You have been saying for years there's nothing between you two," Jessica began. "I don't believe you. I've known you too long Trip, if you don't want to do something, you don't. You like her!"

"That's not the issue," Trip said softly, yet forcefully. "I found out something on Bruce." Trip was attempting to change the subject. "Bruce's file is not with the other personnel files. Thelma said she can get ahold of it tonight or tomorrow after hours. Something's fishy."

Jessica had calmed down from her laughing. "Trip, we suspected during the last case with the first lady there was someone in the first lady's pocket high up in the FBI." Trip nodded. "Were we off; could someone be in Archibald's pocket?" Trip looked at Jessica, shaking his head. Jessica was trying to figure out what she had said wrong. Trip was getting a scowl across his face again. He realized what he was doing.

"I'm sorry, Jessica. It's not you. It's that Archibald Staples. We need to put him down the way you put down a rabid dog! That man has had his hands in more pies . . ."

Trip trailed off. He was furious. Trip wanted to take down Archibald. Not because it would be a big bust, not because it could be a possible career advancement, but simply because Trip was sure Archibald was involved with anything, and everything, illegal.

"Here's what we're going to do," Trip said, snapping out of his thoughts. "We're going to reopen the case on Archibald very quietly. We're going to look into Bruce, very quietly. First though, we have to find the senator. We lose him; we may all lose our jobs."

"John seems to think that they all are tied together," Jessica said quietly. "He's going to talk to his in-laws about Archibald. John seems to think they might know something that would give us a lead."

Trip nodded. "I know," he said.

Jessica looked at the floor and asked the question that had been in her mind ever since John came back into her life. "Trip, what do we do if he finds out?" Trip looked at Jessica sharply.

"About Sam?" Trip asked quietly. Jessica nodded, never lifting her eyes from the floor. She was near tears. She knew if she looked at Trip that she would start to cry. "Well, we might all lose our jobs, and we might lose our friend, but we did what we thought was right at the time. We didn't know Jessica. I think we have to tell him soon. I think he'd rather hear it from us than figure it out on his own."

"What if he's already figured it out?" As soon as the question left Jessica lips, tears began to lightly fall from her face. Jessica worried deep down the reason John had Jessica checking Bruce's IT man's work, and Bruce's guy checking Chet was because John had figured it out. It was either that, or he suspected one of them of some other horrible crime. John did everything for a reason.

She looked up at Trip. Trip's eyes were moist. He set his jaw, but couldn't stop his tears. Jessica got up and left, leaving Trip by himself.

Trip leaned back in his chair and turned it toward the window. He looked in the direction of where John and Sam's old apartment was. He couldn't see it even if it was still standing, but he could see the fire that roared that night in his mind's eye. Trip spoke softly, "What if he has?"

Chapter 35

Jessica hurried down the hallway to the elevator. She took the elevator to the roof. She walked out and stared out over the city. Tears were now flowing freely from her face. All this time John thought that Jessica had been doing things for him. The truth was Jessica had been protecting John because it was her fault Sam was dead and John was alone.

Jessica stomped her foot. It wasn't her fault. She didn't kill Sam, but she hadn't stopped the killer. Why she and Trip hadn't taken Sam's concern more seriously . . . Jessica knew she had to stop asking why. What had happened had happened. What Jessica needed to do was catch the scumbag who had killed her. She shook her head. What she had to do was find the senator. He was still alive, and Sam wasn't.

Jessica looked over the city and couldn't help but smile. John would die if he knew how many times Sam had met Jessica up here just to talk, and most of the time it was about him. It was here that Sam had told Jessica that she thought John had a crush on Jessica. She closed her eyes and could almost hear and see her friend.

"You know he really likes you," she heard Sam say. Jessica opened her eyes and there stood Sam. Jessica shut them for a second, and reopened them. Sam waved at her.

"Why do the two of you keep doing that?" Sam asked.

"The two of who?" Jessica retorted. Sam sighed.

"Really? We're gonna do this now? You're the one seeing people and we're gonna have this discussion?" Sam was smiling broadly. Jessica pinched herself and looked at Sam. Sam had her fingers in her ears, wagging them, and was sticking her tongue out. Jessica laughed at loud. Okay, John had said he saw Sam during the last case, so given the amount of stress she was under it was perfectly reasonable why she was "seeing" Sam.

"Did you work out yet why you're seeing me?" Sam asked. Jessica started to answer but Sam held up her hand. "Could it be, you feel it's your fault I'm dead and now you're feeling really guilty that your falling for my widowed husband?"

"First off, you gave me permission," Jessica began.

"Hold it, Lambada girl," Jessica smiled at the reference to the dance she learned. Sam would always accuse Jessica of learning it just to steal away John. "I never gave you permission. I just told you if something ever happened to me he would make a move on you."

"You act like he just buried you yesterday and was at my door that night!" Jessica retorted.

"So what are you saying?" Sam replied getting very close to Jessica's face.

Jessica replied very loudly, "It's been," she paused. She continued very softly, "three years." Sam held her hand to her ear.

"What was that sweetie, I couldn't hear you?" Sam asked with a smile on her face.

Jessica smiled. "It's been three years." Sam crossed her arms, and still smiling, walked away. She stopped near the edge and looked out over the city. Sam turned back toward Jessica.

"You two better slow down or you'll burn up in the flames of passion," Sam said.

"Okay, okay," Jessica replied. "I get it. You're dead." Sam nodded. "And not coming back."

"Doesn't look that way," Sam replied.

"But, Sam . . ."Jessica began. Sam walked back toward Jessica.

"You know you have accused John of not living, but it seems to me you've not done a whole lot of living yourself. Now admittedly you didn't make the spectacle of yourself he did, but you, Chet, and Trip did all you could do to find my killer? You need to have a life. He's not a bad guy . . . if I do say so myself." Sam grinned broadly at the end of the statement. "It's okay," Sam said quietly. "There's no one I'd rather him be with than you."

Jessica looked down, smiling. When she looked up with tears in her eyes, Sam was gone. Jessica spoke out loud, loudly.

"I know it was all in my head, but just in case it wasn't . . . I miss you!" Jessica turned to go.

As she reached the door, she swore she heard, "I miss you too."

Chapter 36

Luke walked out of the FBI building. He was surprised at how easily he was released. He was sure he would be kept for a couple of days. It made him wonder if they hadn't let him go just so they could follow him.

As he was leaving, he noticed reporters flocking to the building. He thought they were all coming for him, but they all rushed passed him. Luke stopped one of the reporters to find out what was going on.

"You haven't heard?" The reporter asked. "The first lady has been released. It was decided there wasn't enough evidence to hold her on. It also looks like David Geroge is going to be taken to a psychiatric hospital for evaluation. There wasn't any proof that he killed any of the people he was suspected of killing."

The reporter took off and Luke smiled. He headed back toward the building so he could talk to Lisa. As he reached the reporters, Tom, one of the Secret Service agents he had worked with, seemed to appear out of nowhere. He grabbed Luke by the arm and tried to drag him away.

"What do you think you're doing?" Luke asked.

"I'm trying to save you from doing something stupid, but I'm honestly afraid I'm too late," Tom said.

"What are you saying?" Luke asked.

"Luke," Tom began. "Man, you're my friend, but come on. We all know how you have a thing for her. I'm not saying you did anything to the senator, but you have to admit you're one serious suspect. You need to stay away from her. Do you think Archibald is going to let you cozy up to her?"

Luke looked like he had been slapped in the face with that last question.

"Spit it out, Tom, don't dance around it," Luke said. He was angry and Tom knew what he was about to say was only going to make things worse.

"Luke, you're a Secret Service agent. You're supposed to be one of the good guys, not only that, in his eyes, you're just a guy. You're not a powerful senator or anything like that. You don't have the social standing to be in her class. You know and I know you don't have a prayer."

"What if I was a national hero?" Luke asked coyly. Tom stopped dead in his tracks. He closed his eyes and took a deep breath. When he opened them he looked Luke right in the eyes.

"I'm going to pretend I didn't hear that," Tom said, shaking his head. "If, and I stress, IF, you know something about the senator you need to let the right people know." Luke was looking over Tom's shoulder at the first lady who had just come out of the FBI office. Tom stepped into Luke's view. Anger spread over Luke's face. Tom was shaking his head. "Luke, you're playing a dangerous game. Do you think for a minute if I can figure this out that they can't figure this out?" Tom jerked his thumb toward the FBI building with that last statement. Luke set his jaw and looked at Tom. Luke stared at Tom for a minute, shook his head, pulled out his cell phone, put it under the tire of his car, got in and took off, breaking the cell phone. Tom watched him go, shaking his head. He wondered if he would ever see Luke as a free man again.

Chapter 37

Luke drove his car toward Washington, down the New Jersey turnpike. He figured his car was being tracked since the FBI had brought it back from Washington. As he approached Washington, he headed toward Independence Ave, and parked there. He headed towards the Smithsonian Metro station and got on. Luke took the Orange Metro towards Vienna. There he switched over to the Red line and rode it toward Silver Springs. When he arrived at Union Station, Luke got off, and looked around to see if he was being followed. He didn't see anyone, but Luke suspected his clothes had been tagged somehow.

Luke went into different stores in the mall and bought an assortment of clothes. He went into the men's room and found an empty stall. Luke changed clothes and threw the ones he wore out of the FBI building into the trash. He headed out of the mall to find the escape vehicle that Archibald had left him. He went to the spot in the parking lot he was told the vehicle would be in and saw a black SUV. Luke chuckled; Archibald went all out. A young man, he looked about nineteen or twenty, pulled into the spot beside where the SUV was parked. Luke was smiling at what he was thinking.

"Hey," Luke yelled at the young man. "Does your car run okay?"

"Yeah," the guy replied. "It doesn't take much gas or oil."

"Want to trade?" Luke asked. The young man smiled and five minutes later, Luke pulled out in the young man's 1978 Nova. Luke headed toward Virginia down I-395 South. He picked up I-495 East and circled Washington. He picked up MD-295 North and headed toward Baltimore. Luke knew he had just traveled the most out-of-the-way loop possible. He had been looking for a tail, and hadn't found it. Luke smiled to himself. He was sure the surveillance had been hanging back, relying on the bugs he thought were planted on him and his vehicle. He didn't trust Archibald either. Tom may have been right, Luke didn't belong in Staples' circle, and Archibald might have him eliminated. This had all started out with Luke trying to impress Lisa, or Veronica, or whatever she was calling herself today. Luke knew he had to take care of himself. As the car sped toward Baltimore, Luke began to make new plans.

Chapter 38

Two FBI agents, Jeff and Steve, sat in a van in the vicinity of Union Station. They had been conducting surveillance on Luke ever since he left New York. It had been a long day, but they thought it was an easy case, especially since they were supposed to stay out of sight and follow the signals that were being emitted.

The agents had noticed the car tracker hadn't moved from near the Smithsonian for nearly an hour. They switched over to tracking Luke by the small tracer they had planted in his clothes. The signal led them to Union Station and they continued to track him from afar.

After about an hour of the tracker not moving, one of the agents, Jeff, decided to see what was going on. He followed the signal, with a handheld device, into the men's room and found the clothes with the transmitter on it in the trash can. He came back out and told his partner what had happened. The agents fought over who was going to call in and tell "The Hammer" that they had lost Luke.

The two of them argued for fifteen minutes about who would phone this in. They finally decided a fair way to decide who would make the call. Jeff lost at Rock, Paper, and Scissors and had to phone Jessica. He placed the call.

"Agent Hammerstein," Jeff began. "We lost him." Jeff held the phone away from his ear. Jessica was yelling, loudly! He brought the phone back to his ear and listened to the instructions he was given and disconnected the call. Steve looked at Jeff waiting to hear what their next move was.

"We've been called back to New York," Jeff said. "We have to report directly to Agent Hammerstein in the morning." Steve shuddered from the announcement. Jessica had gained a reputation in the agency. According to FBI lore, she could peel the paint off the wall from one of her butt-chewing's.

Later that Night
New York FBI Building

Chapter 39

Trip's office door opened and a man walked inside.
The man looked around and found Trip's fax machine. On
the fax machine was a transmission from Thelma. The man
in Trip's office chuckled. If Trip had the fax sent to his
email, like most people, this interception never would have
been possible. The man studied the fax for a minute,
reached into his pocket and pulled out a cell phone. He
typed out a text and hit send.

The man took the transmission from Thelma and
went over to the shedder. He put the paper into the shedder
and watched the machine tear the document into strips.
About that time, the door to Trip's office opened and a
member of the night cleaning crew started in the office.

"Oh," said the janitor. "I didn't realize anyone was
in here."

"It's ok," said the man. "I was just looking for a file
Trip was supposed to have left me, apparently he forgot.
I'll check with him in the morning."

The janitor smiled and began going about his
business. He opened the bottom of the shedder and
emptied its contents into a drum that would be incinerated
later on that night. The man smiled. He opened the door
and started out. He stopped and turned back toward the
janitor.

"You have a good night," said the man.

"You too, sir," said the janitor. The man headed
down the hallway, to the elevator. As he watched the doors

slide together, he thought about what he would do once he had paid off his debt.

Jessica's Office
New York FBI Building

Chapter 40

Jessica stared at the phone she had just hung up. She had been combing through the paperwork that Bruce's IT guy had come up with. There were over 100 possible places in her mind that Jeremiah Cosby could be stored. She was going over cell phone calls and possible areas they were made from to correspond with possible address of warehouses owed by Archibald. Her search was interrupted when the two agents called her about Luke's disappearance.

She was staring at the receiver, knowing she was wasting her time. What upset her most was that she knew the two agents were griping about what she was going to do to them. They were griping not because they messed up, but because she was a woman. If these two clowns had done this and Trip, or even John, had dressed them down, they wouldn't say a word.

Jessica stuck out her bottom lip and blew air up into her face. There were days she wondered why she put up with this crap. She also wondered what was going to happen now that she and John were seeing each other. Would she be accused of getting special treatment because of their relationship? In her mind, if anyone should get accused of getting special treatment because of their relationship it was John.

Jessica smiled in spite of herself. It did amaze her. John wasn't a great profiler, he could barely turn on a computer, he was an okay marksman, and he wasn't in great shape . . . well . . . he was before the drinking started.

Jessica realized she was smiling a bit too much and shook her head trying to get rid of the mental picture.

Jessica looked out the window of her office at Chet working away, trying to find some lead. Her thoughts drifted back to John. She really couldn't begrudge him anything. At the end of the day, he closed cases. He found leads and read people naturally. Some people could do the same thing, but they had to spend years studying and understanding what they were seeing. With John, he just knew, and the kicker was, he was always right, always!

Jessica scowled a bit. It was what made him so blasted arrogant. Jessica slammed the folder she was working on down on the desk. Chet barely even flinched; he was used to these occasional outbursts. Jessica took in a deep breath. This wasn't John's fault. Jessica knew she was upset that she couldn't solve Sam's murder.

Jessica sat there for a minute staring at her desk. Thinking of Sam had made her think of the Moores. She remembered that John and Bruce were going to visit Arthur and his wife. Jessica wondered if World War III had broken out yet.

The Moore Residence
Virginia

Chapter 41

John was trying to decide which was worse; the ride with Bruce, or going inside to listen to Arthur run him down. John felt the gun in the holster on his hip. He was thinking that maybe he should leave the gun in the car. John didn't think he'd be pushed to the point where he'd shoot Arthur, but he wasn't 100% sure Arthur wouldn't try to go for John's gun and shoot him.

Bruce was watching John and chuckling.

"You know, John," Bruce began. "In kidnapping cases, time is supposed to be of the essence."

John snapped back to reality with that statement. He looked at Bruce, guiltily. John knew he needed to get going on the interview with the Moores, whether he wanted to or not. John reached for the door handle and opened it. He got out of the car and looked back at Bruce, questioningly. Bruce laughed.

"Sorry, buddy," said Bruce. "It's one thing for me to take some verbal shots at you. I really have no want to hear your in-laws rip you a new one."

"I could be a while," replied John.

"I have some games on my cellphone," said Bruce, waving in the air.

John headed towards the door of the house. Bruce watched John disappear inside. Bruce sat in the car laughing. His phone buzzed and he looked at it. He had received a text. Bruce read it thoroughly, and tsked.

"How come I always have to take care of the loose ends?" he asked out loud to no one.

Chapter 42

John walked through the Moore's home. It had been well over three years since he had been there. John didn't necessarily have a bad relationship with his in-laws, he just always felt like they thought Sam could have done better than him; secretly he agreed with the idea.

Madeline walked up to John and looked at him. John started to speak five different times and didn't know what to say. Madeline smiled at him, opened her arms and hugged him. John was stunned. Emotions flowed through him and he began to sob.

"Madeline . . ." He couldn't say anything else.

"Shh," Madeline answered. "It wasn't your fault, son. I know it wasn't your fault." After a minute he gathered himself and broke the hug. Madeline had her hands on John's shoulders.

"You know," Madeline began. "We lost a daughter; we didn't have to lose a son as well."

John looked down at the ground. After everything he had put them through after Sam's death . . . John didn't believe he deserved some of the people in his life. Between his parents, Jessica, Chet, Trip, and Madeline . . . a voice interrupted his thoughts

"So you finally decide to show your face. If I'd have known all I had to do was sue you, I'd have done it three years ago." John knew the voice even before he saw Madeline's face. John turned to face Arthur, Sam's father; the man who blamed John for everything that had happened over the past three years in his life. This wasn't going to be pleasant.

Chapter 43

"Madeline," John said, never taking his eyes off of Arthur. "You might want to leave the room. I believe there may be some things said that shouldn't be said in the presence of a lady."

"John, don't you worry," Arthur responded. "She's heard me call you every name in the book."

"Arthur," John began.

"Save it, John!" Arthur was furious. "You think you can crawl up in a bottle, get my daughter killed, wallow in self-pity, and not have to suffer any consequences! I think it's time you came back to reality, you self-absorbed prima-donna!"

"Prima-donna? You live here in this mansion like you're a member of the lifestyles of the rich and famous, and I'm a prima-donna?" Madeline had been watching the whole exchange and buried her head in her hands with the last remarks. She knew this day had been coming, and so far it hadn't spiraled out of control. She also knew these two alpha dogs would eventually go for each other's throats.

"Here we go," Madeline muttered to herself.

"You got my daughter killed and never a phone call or anything?" Arthur asked. Madeline looked up from her hands. She tried to signal for Arthur to stop, but he ignored her and kept on going. "Oh, my mistake, you did manage to speak to me at the funeral, or do you remember that, Alchy?"

Madeline winched with that last remark.

"I was drunk," John said as calmly as he could. "I was drunk because I had lost my wife." Madeline came up beside John and put her hand on his shoulder to try to comfort him. John patted it. "I was drunk because I was an alcoholic, and I had lost my rock. That was my lowest day, Arthur, and I haven't drank since."

Arthur began to slowly clap; mocking John. "Well whoopty-doo! I lost a daughter and I didn't climb into a bottle!" Madeline cut Arthur a sharp look. "What is it with you, Madeline? It's not like you've never heard me say this before."

"I thought you would get it all out of your system ranting at me, Arthur!" Madeline retorted. "The man had a disease. Excuse me, he HAS a disease. You wouldn't chew out a cancer patient for having cancer."

"A cancer patient didn't kill my daughter!" Arthur was near tears.

Madeline pointed at John as she spoke. "Neither has he! You old fool, he lost his wife!"

"I lost my little girl!" Arthur had tears freely falling down his face. John was close to tears. "He has never lost a child!"

Madeline stared at the floor. She spoke very softly. "He did that day, Arthur. He did that day."

Chapter 44

It took Arthur a second to comprehend what Madeline had just said. He looked at John, then back at Madeline. A look of slow comprehension came over his face.

For John, the world slowed down to a crawl. He saw Arthur's mouth moving, but couldn't understand the words, they were so slow. John noticed Arthur was growing taller. No, that wasn't quite right. John realized he was on the floor. Arthur was bending over him, trying to help him up. Madeline had her hands curled up in fists with her first fingers on her lips. She looked very worried. John tried to ask her what was wrong and realized he couldn't talk.

Sam had been pregnant; that thought kept running through his mind. John thought back to the last morning he saw Sam. He closed his eyes, and suddenly he was in his old New York Apartment.

Chapter 45

John opened his eyes. It was his apartment in New York; the one that had exploded. He was standing in the bathroom in front of the sink. His head . . . hurt. He couldn't think straight. He hadn't felt like this since he quit drinking. John had a hangover. He looked into the mirror in front of him. The John that looked back was one he had not seen in a long, long time. John reached hesitantly to the medicine cabinet and opened it. He looked and saw a small flask. He kept his "emergency wake-up" drink in it. John looked down at the sink, and with all of his strength shut the medicine cabinet door. As he shut the door, he saw Sam in the reflection of the mirror.

"Did you hear me, John?" Sam asked. "Do you think I can go clothes shopping this weekend?" John just stared into the mirror, looking at her. She was so beautiful. He turned around slowly, tears were in his eyes. Sam had a concerned look on her face. "John, tell me you haven't touched your stash in that cabinet!"

John threw his hands up in surrender. "Sam, I swear I haven't touched it." The look of anger and concern left her face and a smile replaced it. John looked very closely. There was something about her. The clothes fit just a bit tighter, there were little signs on her face, but mostly she was so happy. Sam and John had been told by doctors that Sam could never have a child.

John silently berated himself for not noticing when this was actually going on. For days Sam had been talking about shopping for new clothes, something she only did when she needed something for work. John had been so distracted by the job . . . no. It was time to quit lying to himself. John's senses had been dulled by the alcohol. He was constantly drunk these days.

"You're pregnant," John said softly. Sam smiled the biggest smile he had ever seen. She came toward him to hug him; to celebrate. As she walked toward him the whole scene dissolved around him. This wasn't what had happened.

What really happened that morning was John was thinking about the pending Mafia busts. He did take a swig from his flask to dull the pain. He gave Sam a kiss on the cheek, promising they would go shopping this weekend. He had sensed the disappointment in her as he left, but as he looked back, she was smiling at him. She told him good luck. That was the last time he ever saw her alive.

Thelma Hank's Residence
Dale City, Virginia

Chapter 46

Thelma was humming to herself. She was quite happy with herself. Next week Trip was coming to Quantico for a visit. After all of the important meetings, he was hers for the weekend. Thelma was checking her gear for laser tag. It was so nice to find someone else who enjoyed the complexities of the game . . . and Trip wasn't bad looking either!

Thelma laughed to herself. After the match, or matches, they would go out for a nice dinner at a little jazz place they knew. They would have steak, a few drinks, and dance for hours. She wondered what Trip's subordinates would think if they knew how good of a dancer he was. Thelma pulled her head out of the closet quickly. She looked around, thinking she had heard something. After a minute she shrugged. The old house was always creaking and making strange noises.

Suddenly she felt a knee in her back and something against her throat. Something was cutting into her throat. She tried to scream but no noise would come out. The room was spinning. Blackness began to creep in from the outside of her eyesight. Thelma panicked, knowing she only had seconds. She tried to shift her weight to toss her assailant over her. She felt the weight come off her back and heard a thud as her assailant hit the ground. She was stunned as oxygen flooded her lungs. She was gasping as a fist struck her. She fell to the ground and felt hands wrap around her neck. As she began to lose consciousness, she looked up at the face of her attacker.

Bruce stared down at Thelma as she tried to speak.

106

"Shh," he whispered. Thelma was helpless. "Shh," Bruce whispered again. "We don't want anyone hearing you, do we? Why do they always want to say something at the end?" Thelma's eyes shut, and Bruce let go. He rolled her over on her stomach, and straddled her from behind. He hugged her head close to his body.

"I would tell you this is going to hurt me more than it would hurt you, but I'm going to break your neck. That would be lying, and lying is bad." With that, he quickly twisted his arms and a sickening crack made Bruce grin from ear to ear. "Why, Thelma? Why did you have to get involved with my business?"

Bruce drug the body down the stairs. He went into her kitchen, looked around, and smiled. Good, he thought, a gas stove. Bruce disabled the pilot light on the stove, and turned on the burners. He placed a small, homemade contraption on the floor. He had made an igniter using fireworks and a radio controlled car. Bruce chuckled. You can learn anything on the internet. He went outside and sat in the car that was parked a block away. After about 30 minutes he turned on the remote. He started his car, drove to the stop sign, and pressed the drive stick on the remote. The house exploded. Bruce drove the car back towards his hotel. When he got a few blocks away from the hotel, he pulled into an underground parking lot. He parked the car, reached in the glove box and pulled out a license plate. Bruce went to the back of the car and switched the license plate in his hand with the one that was currently on the car. He put the one he just took off back in the glove box. He pulled off the clothes he was wearing and the gloves that were on his hands and placed them in a bag. He quickly put on the running suit he had been wearing when he left the hotel earlier. He threw the bag into a nearby garbage bin. He locked up the car and poured water all over his outfit. He jogged back to the hotel, and the doorman, who had seen him leave an hour ago, waved at him.

"Good run, sir?" The doorman asked.

"Yeah," replied Bruce, gasping for air. "Sitting in a car all day, or behind a desk, dulls the senses. There's nothing like a good run for getting me ready for bed." Bruce headed upstairs chuckling to himself. He had just established an alibi if anyone ever came close to IDing the car. The smile fell from Bruce's face as he thought about having to deal with Trip and John's team soon if they got much closer to the truth.

Moore's Residence
Virginia

Chapter 47

John opened his eyes and looked up at Arthur. Arthur had tears in his eyes. John composed himself and spoke.

"Arthur," John said.

"Yes, John?" Arthur replied.

"If you tell me you love me and try to kiss me I'll shoot you. I do have my gun on me!" Arthur shut his eyes for a minute and a slow smile crossed his face. He opened his eyes and spoke.

"I deserve that, John," Arthur said. Arthur helped John up and into a chair. Madeline was fussing over John. Arthur sat down in a chair from the nearby table. "John . . ." John held up his hand.

"Arthur, I did you wrong at the funeral, and for the past three years." John looked at Madeline. "That goes for you too, Madeline. " John looked at Arthur and took a deep breath. "Arthur, I haven't touched Sam's case because I didn't think I could work it and not start drinking again." John stood and Madeline reached quickly to make sure he would not fall. John smiled at her and got his bearings.

"Arthur, I need your help, and I come with my hat in my hand." Arthur didn't say a word, he just stared at John. "I will tell you everything I know about what happened with the Mafia bust and Sam's death. I'll see if I can get Chet and Jessica to fill in any blanks that I don't know yet." Arthur remained quiet and kept staring at John. Madeline looked at Arthur, picked up the folded newspaper nearby, and then slapped him on the shoulder with it. Arthur jumped, startled.

"No, Madeline," John said, holding up his hand. "I have one more thing to offer; the golden goose." Both Madeline and Arthur turned their heads slowly toward John in anticipation of what he was going to say. Tears were forming in Madeline's eyes. John nodded at Madeline, and Madeline took Arthur's hands in hers.

"Spit it out, boy," Arthur demanded. "I'm not getting any younger!"

John looked down at the floor and spoke very softly. "I'll open Sam's case, and I'll stay on it until it's solved. If it's the last thing I do, I'll find Sam's killer."

Chapter 48

Arthur stepped up to John and stuck out his hand. Madeline let out a deep breath. John held up one finger.

"Uh, not yet, Arthur, I'll do all of this on three conditions," John said.

Arthur raised an eyebrow. He nodded for John to continue.

John held up one finger. "First off, I need to find Jeremiah." Arthur nodded. "I'll start Sam's case as soon as I finish finding the senator. To do that I need you to tell me everything you can about Archibald."

"Done!" Arthur exclaimed.

John reached into his coat and pulled out three folded pieces of paper and handed them to Arthur. Arthur took a look at them. He reached into his pocket to get his reading glasses. He took the papers over to the table and looked them over.

"Do you know who owns these loans?" Arthur asked, looking up from the papers.

"I have a pretty good idea," replied John. "See, Arthur, two friends of mine, and of Sam's, owe that money. The third one, just the name, I have a hunch also owes. I need it verified." Arthur frowned. "I could have taken care of the problem, but I can't touch any of Sam's money." Arthur looked at John. "I'm not asking you to lift the lawsuit, just take the money out of Sam's trust and fix it."

Arthur looked over the papers again and shook his head. He picked up one of the sheets and looked at it, and then at John. John shrugged.

"Would it help you to know he's in a program?" John asked. Arthur slowly nodded his head. He reached into his pocket and pulled out his cell phone. "I have a counter offer," he said to John. He got up and walked out of the room for a minute. Madeline walked over to the table and looked at the papers. She gasped and looked at John.

"What is he doing, Madeline?" John asked.

"Well, John Fowler, you should know Arthur well enough to know that he's going to make sure they can't be used, or used any more, if that's what's going on." She shook her head and looked directly at John. "He's going to fix it." John looked confused. "He will buy a group of loans with this one in it," gesturing with one of the papers. "The other loan," Madeline continued looking over the paper. "Arthur has a few deals he's been holding on to that would benefit the owner of this loan," Madeline said with a smile on her face. "He'll make the loan part of the deal and Arthur will make it go away. Arthur will also have the other loan forgiven."

John was stunned. "Madeline, that's not what I was asking for!"

Madeline smiled at John. "John, we have more than we'll ever need, but never enough to bring back our daughter." Madeline let that sink in. "He's a different man now, John. He lost two people with her death."

Chapter 49

John stood there for a moment, not trusting his ears with what he had just heard.

"Madeline," John began softly.

Madeline walked over to John and hugged him. "He loves you too, John. He loves you too," Madeline repeated softly.

John stood there for a moment. He looked around the house, and noticed it was now very late. He wasn't sure how long he had been out earlier.

"Uh, Madeline, where's Bruce?" John asked.

"Oh, him," Madeline said with a shudder. "He always looks at me like . . . like he hates me, but you never see it on his face. Does that make sense?" Madeline shook her head thinking about Bruce. "We told him you were staying the night here. He said he needed some rest. He took the car and headed back to a hotel. How that boy came from Jeremiah, I'll never know."

Arthur walked back into the room smiling. "You were right about the name. He's way in over his head. The other two, I've fixed both of them John. First thing in the morning, they'll fax me a paid in full sheet that you can take to both of them." Arthur looked very sternly at John. "You make sure that boy NEVER gets in bed with him again! You understand?" John nodded. "Now what's number three?"

John shook his head. "That was it. I wanted you to fix the two, the other name was three." John stuck out his hand to shake. Arthur looked John up and down.

"No deal, son," Arthur said. John was confused. "You said three things, so I need a third. How about this? I drop the lawsuit." John's mouth dropped and Arthur smiled, quite pleased with himself. "I actually had my lawyer drop the lawsuit when I was making the calls earlier."

John didn't know what to say.

"Oh, come off it, son!" Arthur said. "I don't want that money, and you've been through enough. All I ever wanted was the greatest detective I've ever seen to look into Sam's death." John still didn't know what to say. Tears were beginning to form in his eyes. John noticed one in Arthur's. John's slow grin that irritated so many slowly crept across his face.

"John," Arthur began, trying to look stern. "Don't start with your know-it-all thing right now!" John held out his hand for Arthur to shake. Arthur reached out and took John's hand. The grin on John's face broke out into a full-fledge smile. John pulled Arthur in and hugged him. Madeline rolled her eyes.

"I'm so glad you two Alpha dogs got that out of your system," Madeline said.

Arthur and John broke their hug. John looked at Arthur.

"So that's where Sam got it from, I just always assumed it was you, Arthur," John said.

"I get that all the time," replied Arthur.

Madeline harrumphed, and left the room. She was smiling broadly, but the two men couldn't see her.

Chapter 50

John and Arthur sat down at the kitchen table. They began to talk about Archibald Staples. Arthur told John about every deal that he knew Archibald had been involved in. Arthur talked for two hours. John knew most everything that Arthur talked about. As John listened his hope for finding the senator began to fade. Since the incident in Kentucky nearly twenty-five years ago that Archibald's daughter was involved in, there was nothing illegal that could be found on Archibald. While Archibald was making millions of dollars legally in the United States, there was more income than there should be.

RICO agents and tax lawyers had looked into Archibald, but that was a dead-end. Archibald was paying taxes on everything. Whatever Archibald was doing, it was out of the country. If the Senator was being held captive outside of the country . . . there was nothing John could do about that.

John had just about decided to go to bed when Arthur mentioned something in passing. John's head snapped up and he stared at Arthur. Arthur thought about what he said and looked confused.

"Say that again," John said, excitement beginning to run through him.

"I said that the worst thing is, Archibald got his start from his in-laws and then, after his wife died, he bought them out," Arthur repeated. Arthur looked very confused.

"Arthur, think very carefully," John began. "The business he bought out, what happened to it?"

Arthur leaned back in his chair. "Well, he closed down the company. He once told me he left the warehouses empty as a testament to his wife. I couldn't figure out if he meant his life was empty without her, or they had an empty marriage." Arthur stared off into space thinking about what he had just said.

John rolled his eyes at the amateur psychologist hour. He put his hands on Arthur's shoulders. Arthur came back to Earth. John was trying to keep from shaking with excitement.

"Arthur, the buildings? Whose name were they put in?"

"Oh, that," began Arthur. "He put them in a shell company that Veronica controlled for tax reasons . . . oh . . . . OH!" Arthur's mouth dropped when he realized what he had told John and what it could possibly mean. He looked at John and understood now what his daughter meant about there were times you could literally see the locks tumbling in John's head.

John was positive where Senator Cosby was being held. He jumped up ready to go find him. That's when his cell phone went off, and chaos broke loose.

Chapter 51

John looked at his phone. The first thing he noticed was the time, 2:30 am. The second thing he noticed was who the call was from, Jess. John looked at Arthur who nodded and headed out of the room. John smiled as he answered the phone.

"So let me guess, you woke up from a dream about me and wondered if there was any way possible I could be as good as the dream. Well, the answer is no, Jess. The real me is better than any dream you'd ever have." John was smiling. He was very proud of himself at that moment.

There was silence at the other end. John looked at the phone to make sure the call hadn't been disconnected. He saw it hadn't and put the phone back to his ear.

"Jess?" He asked. "Jess, are you there."

"Agent Fowler," Jessica responded. John's heart leapt into his throat. The last time he had heard Jessica use that tone . . . Tears rushed to John's eyes. John started looking for Arthur. He stepped back and could see through the doorway that both Arthur and Madeline were in the living room. Apparently Madeline had fallen asleep on the couch. They were both safe and Jessica was on the phone, that only left Chet and Trip.

"Jess," John began. He took a deep breath and blurted out. "Who's dead, Trip or Chet?"

The second of silence was almost unbearable for John.

"Neither, John," Jessica replied. "John, I'm on my way to Dale City with both Chet and Trip." John's head was spinning trying to put all the pieces together. He had a million questions.

"There has been an explosion and a death of someone who worked at Quantico," Jessica stated. "Chet built a program that would automatically inform me of cases that were similar to an open case I have."

John's mind was reeling. An open case of Jessica's . . . there was only one case that Jessica had that John knew was open . . .

"Agent Fowler," Jessica began and that's when it hit John. She had referred to him as Agent Fowler. The last time she referred to him as Agent Fowler was when he was a suspect in his wife's death . . . the only case that John knew Jessica had open. John sat down in the chair behind him without even looking. Did this mean . . .

"Jess," John began very quietly. "Jess, am I a suspect?"

"No," Jessica replied quickly.

John understood. Jessica was not alone with just Chet and Trip. She was trying to tip him that this case might involve someone in his wife's death. This case might have the same killer. John's mouth went dry. His heart began to race. He took a deep breath.

"Agent Hammerstein," John began with a smile on his face. "I bet you about dropped the phone when I answered it the way I did." John heard a light chuckle on the other end.

"Yes, yes I did," she replied.

"You're already in Virginia I take it?" John asked.

"Yes I am," Jessica replied.

"A higher up from Quantico is with you?" John asked.

"Very observant, Agent Fowler," Jessica responded.

"Does he know about the link between this murder and my wife's?" John asked very quietly.

"No," Jessica replied. John was puzzled. He wasn't for sure what was going on. "Do you remember Thelma Hanks?" Jessica asked.

John lowered his head. He did remember Thelma. He knew Trip was in love with her, and she was with him. John stood up. "I do. Jess, text me the address, I'm on my way." John disconnected, told the Moores he had to leave, and asked to borrow a car. Arthur tossed John the keys, and John ran outside to the car. As he was getting in the car, his mind was spinning. He had a lead on the senator and now, after all this time, he might have a lead on his wife's killer. A smile spread across John's face. While he was sad for the death of Thelma and for Trip, he couldn't help but be excited to finally be on the trail of the one person in the world he wanted to see dead.

Thelma Hank Residence
Dale City, Virginia

Chapter 52

As John pulled up to what was left of the address he was texted, he couldn't help to think back to the night of Sam's death. He stared at the burning wreckage that had been Thelma's house. It reminded him of that night as his apartment burnt in the New York night. He had lain on the ground that night, knocked back by the explosion. He had wanted to get up and run to his apartment, but he had been a FBI agent for too long. He knew Sam was gone. He stared that night at the fire that burned against the clear sky. John shook the memories from his head.

John got out of the car and scanned the area. He saw Jess, Chet and Trip. He examined Trip closely. John wasn't 100% sure of Trip and Thelma's relationship, but he knew they loved each other. That was obvious to John by the body movements Trip had at work when she was mentioned, and here, at what remained of her home. John sighed deeply. This was going to be rough. John knew better than anyone what Trip was going through right now. Trip was standing apart from Jessica and Chet. John took a deep breath and started toward him. Jessica saw John and tried to stop him, but John waved her off.

"Chet," Jessica said to him, not even looking at Chet but watching John head toward Trip. "We're about to see massive fireworks, one way or another."

John walked up to Trip and stood there quietly. Trip felt John at his shoulder, but ignored him. Trip gazed into the fire. John counted mentally to 100, and when Trip still hadn't acknowledged him, John spoke.

"Trip," John began. "Don't hold this in."

Trip turned to John, anger spreading quickly across his face.

"So you go to one counseling session and you think you can help save the world?" Trip spoke quietly, but very angrily. John didn't say anything. "You have no idea what I'm going through. You don't know my relationship with Thelma. I know you think you know. I know you think you know everything with you special 'abilities.' For God's sake man! Why did they even let you in the FBI? You're not a profiler, you're not a forensic scientist, and you can't even tell others how you know the things you know! You can just watch someone and deduce it in your head! Well here's something you don't know, Mr. Know-It-All! I killed her! I asked her to do something for me and now she's dead!"

Trip began to tremble. John knew what was coming next, and now realized how little he had thought through his plan. Trip was going to need a shoulder to cry on, and John really didn't think there was any way he was going to get around the awkwardness of this moment. It was at that second Jessica, who had been watching the whole thing and began walking toward them during their exchange, hugged Trip. Trip broke down and began to sob. Chet did his best to stand in a way that shielded others from seeing what was going on. After a minute or so, Trip regained his composure, and Jessica released Trip. Trip nodded his thanks toward Jessica, and looked at John sheepishly. Trip began to speak, but John held up his hand.

"Trip," John began. "If anyone knows about saying things they regret in these situations, well, you're looking at him." Trip nodded. "Now, what do you have facts-wise about what you just told me?"

Trip shook his head. He looked at the remains of Thelma's house and looked back at John. He looked hopeless. John had seen that look before. It had stared at him in a mirror for three years. John placed his arm on Trip's shoulder. Trip blew out a breath and tried to hold it together.

"I don't know anything for sure, John, I just know what I think," Trip replied. He was on the verge of losing it with each word he spoke, but he managed to hold it together. John nodded, and looked at the burning building. John felt the feelings of loss start to build in him, but instead of fighting them, he let them come. While John was looking toward the building, Jessica moved to where she was looking Trip directly in the face, with a questioning look on her face. Trip shook his head no, quickly, and Jessica let it go. Trip walked over to John and stood beside him, both men looking at the fire.

Chapter 53

Chet and Jessica walked up behind the two men. John spoke, softly.

"Trip, I don't know what you felt for Thelma, and it's not my place to judge," John began. "Tonight, you've had something ripped away from you. Tonight, you've been told something is over that you never had a chance to fight for. I'd like to tell you that eventually that feeling goes away. That would be a lie."

Tears were in Trip's eyes. John turned toward him. Jessica and Chet stood there silently. Both thought they should be uncomfortable with the situation, but they weren't. Jessica had the craziest thought that they were becoming a family. Not the Christmas card kind. More like the dysfunctional get Uncle George out of the potato salad at the reunion type of family. Nonetheless they were becoming a family.

"I'm going to tell you what I think," John began. "I think you two had an arrangement that worked for both of you. I think both of you wanted more, but you were good with where you were." Trip continued to look at the building, tears streaming down his face. He was barely nodding, but he was confirming everything John said. "Trip, you were both happy. Hold on to that. Remember that, relish it. You hold onto that when you have these moments where you think your world is about to come crashing around you. When it's late at night and you think you might go crazy from the questions of what more could I have done, remember that you were happy. Remember that Thelma loved life, and lived it. Remember that she wouldn't want you to stop living your life. Remember that you're not dead, and if you don't go on, then that would make Thelma unhappy. Remember to be happy."

Trip turned to John, nodding as tears streamed down his face. Against his better judgment, John hugged

Trip. When they broke the embrace, Jessica put her arm on John's shoulder. She had read between the lines of what John said. While this was Trip's moment, and everything should be about him, she knew that John had his walls down. She knew they needed John if they were to solve the cases in front of them. Jessica silently admonished herself, but she did what she knew she needed to do.

"You know you have that too, John," Jessica said.

John squared his jaw and fought back the tears. He turned to Jessica, with anger in his eyes. Not at her, but at what he had done.

"Do I, Jess?" John asked. "Do I really? I mean the two of you were best friends and I didn't notice. I am known for my 'gift'. I mean right or wrong, what Trip said a few minutes ago was spot on. I am not a forensic scientist, I am not a psychologist, or a profiler, or anything that is glamorous. I'm an old school detective that notices things no one else does. I didn't even notice you and my wife were best friends. I didn't even notice that I was too far gone to notice! I was so absorbed in myself and my next drink that I missed the obvious!"

"That was my fault," Trip said quietly. Shock hit Chet's face when he heard those words. He turned toward Trip. The color drained out of Jessica's face. She looked down at the ground hoping to avoid John's explosion. John didn't explode. He slowly turned toward Trip with mild amusement on his face.

"Do you want to run that one by me again, Boss?" John asked.

Chapter 54

"I was concerned about you," Trip began. "You were so far into the mob, and the drinking . . . " Trip let the sentence trail off, as he looked back toward the house. He kept looking at the house as he continued.

"I needed to test you, so I asked Jessica to start meeting with Sam," Trip said. He had a quick laugh and shook his head. He looked at John. "She was just like you, John." John looked confused. "Sam knew what was up quickly. She came to me and thanked me for caring about you. I put in a request to pull you off the case six months before the bust. It was denied. You were in so deep and the thought was you could bring down so many . . ." Trip looked over at the burning remains of Thelma's house and shook his head. He collected himself and continued. "The higher ups thought the risk was justified. They only cared about the bottom line. John, you were expendable. It was almost like they were trying to get rid of you."

Trip blew out a breath. He knew he had to be careful. There were so many things that John didn't know. All Trip had to do was let the wrong piece of information slip and everything would crumble like a house of cards. The problem was part of him didn't care. All of these secrets . . . had all of these secrets gotten Sam and Thelma killed? He had it with all the secrecy. Trip turned toward John. It was time to face the music, it was time to tell John everything that had happened and let the chips fall where they may. He started to open his mouth when John held up his hand.

"Listen," John began. "You've been through something very traumatic. I know all three of you are keeping something from me, a lot of somethings." Trip, Jessica, and Chet looked like they had been hit in the stomach with a baseball bat. The air had been knocked out of them. John smiled to himself. He knew he could get all three of them to tell him everything right here and now, but it wasn't the time. They had to find the senator. Then they could deal with Sam, and Thelma.

"You really thought the three of you could keep whatever it is from me," John said. "It's been screaming at me from the beginning you haven't been telling me the whole story. I admit, I have been a little rusty, and it took me a bit to put all of the pieces together, but it's obvious there is more than what you have been telling me. Whatever it is, I'm sure you all did whatever you did with the best intentions, but we don't have time for all of this right now. I have a lead on the senator." John turned to Chet.

"Chet, Arthur told me there is supposed to be a company that Archibald took over." John said. "It was owned by his in-laws. The company is placed in a group of shell corporations that is owned by Archibald's daughter. Supposedly there is one building that still physically exists."

Chet nodded. John watched Chet and realized the spot he had just put Chet in. John smacked his head in front of them all. The three of them looked at John like he was crazy.

"I'm sorry, Chet, I forgot to tell you," John began. "Your loan to Archibald has been paid off so you don't have to tell him what we found out."

As the look of shock registered in the eyes of his friends, John rocked back on his heels. You know, he thought to himself, sometimes it's just hard being me.

126

Chapter 55

Chet stammered and stuttered and didn't know what to say. John decided it was time to go ahead and let his other friend off the hook. He turned toward Jessica.

"Jess," John began. "Did you know that Archibald had just bought out the company that owned your private loans for college?" Jessica, who had a look of shock on her face from the bomb John had just dropped regarding Chet, began to look very confused. She started to stammer and seemed very flustered.

"I am not a mole!" Jessica exclaimed, pointing down with her index finger for emphasis as she spoke very quietly but fiercely.

"Of course you're not," John said. "And neither is Chet for that matter."

Trip looked absolutely stunned. Some of the biggest secrets Trip had ever been a part of and John had figured them out in a little over a week.

"Oh come on!" John exclaimed. "I mean you three have been obviously trying to hide something from me since this whole thing started. Ever since you and Chet," pointing at Jessica and Chet, "stormed into my apartment you've been trying to hide something from me. It's like holding up a sign. I don't know what it is that you all are hiding, but I know you two are not moles. I know how everything is supposed to look."

John paused a second and looked into the fire. He turned and faced his friends and continued. "I know someone went to an awful lot of trouble to set things up in a way to make me waste my time looking into something that wasn't there. I know there is a mole in the FBI. I am not for sure who it is. I do have a pretty good idea, but I know it's not you two," John paused and looked at Chet. John rocked his head side-to-side, and decided to amend what he had said. "Well, Chet is, but he's a double mole set up by you, I believe," John said pointing at Trip. "My guess is Chet is running everything he is passing to Archibald by you." John paused.

Trip's jaw was nearly on the ground. "Un-freaking-believable," Trip said softly. "You haven't been around in three years physically, and the year before that you were so drunk, you didn't notice anything. We bring you back in and you figure everything out. Un-freaking-believable."

John nodded. He looked down at the ground. Everything could wait until after the case, except for one thing. There was one thing he had to know. He lifted his head and looked at Jessica. There were tears in his eyes. Jessica looked back at him with uncertainty. After all the things he had figured out in his own special way, there was one thing he needed confirmed.

"Did you know, Jessica?" John asked. "Did you know Sam was pregnant?"

Chapter 56

Tears came to Jessica's eyes. She sucked her upper lip in, and slowly shook her head back and forth.

"Oh, John," she said, barely above a whisper. "Oh, no. Oh, John." Jessica started to lose her composure. She placed her right hand over her mouth with her index finger over her upper lip, her thumb cupping her chin, leaving her hand extending out. She looked at John and then looked away. She did this several times, each time trying to speak and not being able to. Chet looked at John with absolute shock. Trip stared off into the fire, slowly shaking his head.

"She said you didn't know, John . . . she said you didn't know," Jessica was speaking barely above a whisper, her voice breaking from the emotion.

"I didn't know until a few hours ago," John replied with tears streaming down his face. "I didn't know until Madeline let it slip during my argument with Arthur."

"I didn't find out until after her autopsy was performed," Trip said, never looking away from the fire. "It was my call not to tell you, Jessica and Chet wanted to, but I said no." Trip turned toward John. "John, you have to understand after all you'd been through . . . " Trip couldn't continue. He stood there shaking his head. Trip's face was filled with sadness; not only from his loss, but from the past finally beginning to catch up with him.

Chet stepped in between everyone to stand directly in front of John. Jessica stepped back to give him room.

"Are you okay?" Chet asked.

"I'm not okay, Chet," John replied. "I'm not okay, because I should have known she was pregnant. She couldn't share the one moment in her life she had always hoped for." John paused, gathered himself, and continued. "The one moment that she had dreamt of more than anything in her life and I took it away from her. All she

129

ever wanted to do was to have kids and have my support. Me and my alcoholism snatched away my wife's greatest dream, and I'll have to live with that for the rest of my life."

Chet repeated the words John had said in his head, and began to smile. John noticed the smile and gave him a confused and slightly angry look. Chet just smiled broadly.

"John, you didn't say you were responsible for her death," Chet said, with a grin.

"I know," John replied angrily. He stopped and thought for a second. Chet had him and wasn't about to let go. He pressed on.

"Why?" Chet asked. John looked at him, confused. "Why did you not say you were responsible?'

"Because I'm not," John replied, irritated with being questioned. Jessica shoved Chet aside. She had a vicious grin on her face. John's eyes widened. The last time he had seen that look on her face he had watched a suspect confess to every crime he had ever committed in his entire life.

"Step out of the way boys; it's time for a pro to finish this!" Jessica said with a smile.

Chapter 57

"Mr. Fowler," Jessica began. "The last time you and I discussed your wife's death at length, you said you were responsible for her death." John nodded. "Are you changing you story?"

"Do you mean when I was being interrogated by you about the explosion? John asked. Jessica nodded. John wasn't sure what was going on, but he didn't like it. "Jess, what do," John began, but Trip cut him off.

"Uh-uh, buddy," Trip said. "You're my agent now, and I am ordering you to answer her questions!"

John's eyebrows arched up in surprise. Trip and Chet came to either of side of Jessica. Jessica continued.

"Are. You. Changing. Your. Story?" Jessica emphasized each word of her question. Her eyes were dancing.

"Well," John stammered. He was in new territory. When Jessica had interrogated him last time he had been drunk. As bad as the interrogation was before, he never realized how intimidating she could be when she was in the zone, and right now, Jessica "The Hammer" Hammerstein was in the zone, and John Fowler was right in the center of her crosshairs. John swallowed, and tried to regain his composure.

"I didn't kill her if that's what you're asking, Jessica," John replied.

"Who did?" Jessica fired back quickly.

"I don't know," John said, extending his hands and shrugging.

"Why not?" Jessica asked.

"Because I haven't investigated the crime?" John responded, almost answering the question with a question.

"Why not?" Jessica was rapid firing questions at John. John looked extremely confused.

"Answer her!" Trip demanded.

"Because, I haven't been an FBI agent." John responded, angrily.

"Why not?" Jessica asked this question a little slower, slightly emphasizing each word.

"Because I quit!" John spat.

"Why?" Jessica asked quietly.

"Because I couldn't save her! Is that what you want to hear? Some nut killed her and I couldn't save her!" John screamed. Tears were in his eyes for what felt like the hundredth time that evening. John lowered his head and nodded slowly. "Because I couldn't save her," John said, barely above a whisper. Chet raised his hand, smiling, and Jessica gave him five without even looking at him. Trip nodded, jaw clenched.

"Do I have this to look forward to?" Trip asked John very softy but directly.

John couldn't help himself and barked out a laugh.

"No, Trip, not if you let people into your life and you deal with your emotions like a grown-up," John said, chuckling.

"So that's what the problem was," Jessica deadpanned. She had never broke eye contact with John and still had the grin on her face she had during the entire interrogation session. "You're still not a grown-up, so you never had a chance."

John smiled a fake "ha-ha" smile at her. "What do you want me to say?" John asked. "You were right and I was wrong?"

Jessica crossed her arms. "That would be a start," she replied. Chet reached over and tapped Trip's shoulder behind Jessica's back. Trip looked over at Chet and saw Chet's head gesture for them to walk away. They strolled away together, neither Jessica nor John noticing them leaving.

"You should probably get to searching on that building John was talking about," Trip said.

"Will do, Boss," Chet replied. "Boss, did you catch what John said about a mole."

Trip nodded, never breaking his stride.

"I did, Chet," Trip replied. "Let's find the senator and then we go full bore after Sam and Thelma's killer. I have a feeling Jessica's right and they are the same person, but not a word to John; not yet. I need to be sure before I tell him what I suspect. He didn't like that I earlier implied that Bruce was a sociopath, and he won't like it at all that I think he might have had something to do with these killings."

Chet nodded as he walked. The two men came to a FBI van and Chet started to get in to find the building Trip had mentioned. Chet stopped and looked back at Trip.

"I'm sorry, Trip," Chet said, and climbed into the van. Trip turned back and looked at the house.

"Me too, Chet," he said barely above a whisper. "Me too. I love you, Thelma; rest in peace. I promise you, we'll get him Thelma. We'll get him, and he'll pay!'

Chapter 58

John and Jessica were still standing there facing each other. Jessica's smile was turning into a smirk, and it was causing John to laugh.

"I don't think you should be so proud that you broke down a fellow agent who was under orders to give you all the answers that you wanted," John said.

"Did you tell the truth?" Jessica asked.

"Yeah," John replied looking at the ground. He looked back up at Jessica. "Yeah, I did. I want you to know I'm not mad about you not telling me about Sam." Jessica's expression changed to concern.

"What happened exactly?" Jessica asked.

"Madeline kinda let it slip. Arthur and I were arguing like four year olds. I said I lost my wife, he yelled back that he had lost his child, and that's when Madeline blurted out, so did he, or something like that. I think she was tired of me not knowing. I don't think Arthur knew from the way he reacted. I didn't have time to question him about it. See, you might say I," John paused looking a little sheepish. He glanced around to make sure no one was close and leaned in. "Passed out." Jessica's eyebrows shot up in surprise. The hint of a smile played on the corners of her mouth. John smiled and continued.

"I guess I had an episode or something. I remembered the last morning I saw her before I went to work." Jessica crossed her arms and listened intently. John continued. "I noticed, in the dream, or episode, or whatever it was, I noticed that she was pregnant. But that's not what really happened. The morning I left she was trying to drop hints, and Jess," he paused. Emotions were running through him again, but each time they came, they were less and less powerful. He shook his head and then looked Jessica right in the eye. "Jessica, I missed them. I was so drunk, hung-over, or self-absorbed, I missed it."

John let out a deep breath and asked the question that had haunted him for three years.

"Jess," he asked. "Did I miss something about her death? Did I see something and not catch it. Did she die because of it?" Jessica brought up her finger quickly to John's face. She had the most serious look John had ever seen on her face.

"John Edward Fowler!" She admonished him. "You do not get to reopen that door! You do not get to undo all the progress you made! Do you understand me? If you missed something, yes, it's tragic, but how do you think we feel?" John looked at her, confused. "John, the three of us cared about Sam as well. She was part of the family. Here's the thing, if you missed it, then so did the three of us!" She waved her arm around at the two men she thought were standing behind her. It was then she noticed that they were alone. "Where'd they go?"

"I've noticed that they do that quite often," John began. "They leave when they think you and I are about to have a moment." Jessica raised her left eyebrow and smiled slyly.

"Are we about to have a moment, Mr. Fowler?" Jessica asked walking towards him. John swallowed and looked around at his surroundings.

"While I think the fire is a nice romantic backdrop, it might be a little tasteless to have a moment here," John replied.

Jessica stopped midstride. The smile fell from her face and she pursed her lips together, looking a bit sheepish. She pointed with her thumbs over her shoulder as she spoke.

"So I guess we should probably go and try to find Chet. We should probably see if he found the building, and make sure Trip is okay," Jessica said, trying to recover from the embarrassing moment. John nodded and Jessica started to turn to walk away. John followed her.

"I'm not sure whether that's hot, or scary," John said. Jessica turned midstride on the balls of her feet. She had an inquisitive look on her face. She raised an eyebrow questioningly.

"You know," John began, "the fact you're hot and bothered at a murder scene as the house behind us burns to the ground." John pointed toward the house burning with his thumb as he spoke. Jessica pursed her lips, shrugged with her thumbs in the pockets of her jeans. She tilted her head and spoke quietly.

"Maybe it's scary hot," Jessica said. She spun around and headed toward the van. John watched her walk away, replaying the words in his head. He started to speak several times, gesturing each time he started. He stopped, knowing he looked like he was having a fit. He smiled as he watched her walk away. He was pretty sure he was falling in love. Surprisingly, the thought didn't bother him. John looked toward the burning house. The sight of it did bother him. He sighed and headed toward the van.

Chapter 59

Chet was working furiously in the van as Jessica and John approached. Jessica started to speak, but Trip shook his head quickly. Chet was grinning as his fingers were flying. After a minute he spun around in the chair he was sitting in as a printer was beginning to print. Chet pulled the page off the printer and handed it to John.

"There you go, Boss," Chet said. "This is the only physical building left from the company you described to me. It's in Baltimore on the docks. There are hundreds of warehouses down there."

John pulled out his cell. He called Bruce.

"Bruce," John said. "It's John, get dressed. I think we know where your father is. Chet figured it out. See you in a few minutes."

John turned toward his team and Trip. He looked at each one and took a deep breath.

"Is this," John said, nodding toward the dying fire, "the exact same MO as Sam?" Trip, Chet, and Jessica all looked at each other. Jessica spoke up.

"We won't know for sure until we get into autopsy," Jessica replied.

John's chewed on his bottom lip for a second waiting for Jessica to tell him more, but after a moment he realized he was going to have to come out and ask.

"What exactly are they looking for in autopsy that would connect the two cases, besides the obvious?" John asked. Jessica glanced at Trip and looked down at the ground. Trip muttered something and walked off, tears running down his face. Chet grabbed John by the arm.

"John," Chet admonished. "This isn't about you!" John was stunned at his friend. All John had thought about was solving the case. He never took a second to realize that Trip was still grieving.

"Since you've gotten to this crime scene you've managed to make every conversation about you! Trip is grieving. I know you think you're about to find Thelma and Sam's killer, but if it were you, knowing what you know, do you think it's best for Trip to jump right back into the work, or maybe, just maybe, should we give him a little bit of time to deal with it?"

Chet turned and left John and Jessica. Chet went over to Trip and began to quietly talk to him. John was looking at the ground.

"I can be a real insensitive jerk, can't I?" John asked quietly.

"Yeah, you can," Jessica answered. Her arms were crossed, and the look on her face told John she was 100% serious. John sighed. Jessica uncrossed her arms and reached out and took John's hand. "You obsess when you see a puzzle. You move mountains trying to figure something small and simple out. But . . . you can also be very sweet and thoughtful, but when you get wrapped up in a case . . . " She let the thought hang. John knew what she meant. She pointed toward his car. "Go. Go save the senator, I'll call the local LEOs and have them ready as back-up. Call me."

Jessica did a double-take of the car. John smiled.

"Bruce has the FBI car, the Moores loaned it to me," John said.

"I get to drive it at some point, right?" Jessica asked, with a sly smile on her face.

John nodded and took off. Jessica sighed. She pulled out her cell phone and began making the calls for John's back-up.

Chapter 60

Jessica finished her phone calls and headed over to Trip and Chet.

"Trip," Jessica said as she walked up to her two friends. "John didn't mean to be . . ." Jessica paused, searching for the word. A smile came to Trip's face.

"So John?" Trip offered. Jessica smiled. "It's okay, Jessica. We all know John; he means well. He probably thinks solving this case will make things better for me. He doesn't think about human emotions the way we do. I honestly think it has something to do with his 'skill,'" Trip used air quotes. He continued. "You all know we're gonna have to tell him that someone broke Sam's neck."

"He already suspects," Chet said. Trip and Jessica both looked at Chet. "Remember, Stephen's interview with John?" Chet and Jessica both nodded, and then looked at each other at the same time. They both turned toward Chet. Chet looked confused.

"Does John know that interview was taped?" Jessica asked. Chet shrugged.

"I tried to cover some things when I slipped, but I suspect he does," Chet answered. "Either way, he already said fire is a good way to hide evidence," Chet glanced at the fire. "How big of an explosion do you think we'll get to witness when he finds out someone broke her neck and then burned the body to cover it?" Chet glanced over at Trip. Jessica looked like she could strangle Chet. "I'm so sorry, Boss, I wasn't thinking." Trip waved it off.

"Something doesn't feel right about all of this," Trip said. "Stephen just showing up to conduct John's reinstatement session . . ." Trip trailed off, lost in thought. "Chet, can you do a search on Stephen's financials and make sure no one can trace it?" Chet looked insulted. "I'm sorry, Chet, we just need to be extra careful on this one."

"Do you think Stephen and Bruce are working together Trip?" Jessica asked. Chet's mouth dropped open. Trip didn't know how to react to the question.

"I mean, it's obvious we three think Bruce had something to do with Thelma's death and now I'm beginning to wonder about Sam's death. Are the two of them working together, or possibly even for someone?"

Trip thought about it for a moment. "I honestly don't think Bruce would work for anyone, unless it suited Bruce. Let's get to Baltimore, I don't want to take a chance we're right about Bruce and he tries to do something to John."

The three ran to their car and headed toward the address Chet had found. As the car left the crime scene Trip took one last look at Thelma's house.

Jeremiah Cosby
At an Undisclosed Location

Chapter 61

Jeremiah had been sitting quietly for what he felt was an eternity. He had no idea what time it was. He was tired, hungry, and his body was cramping from being tied in the same position for what seemed like days. Also, he really needed to go to the bathroom. Jeremiah swallowed and decided he had to say something or he was going to wet himself.

"Hello," he called out.

The room was quiet. Jeremiah listened but didn't hear anyone. Wait, what was that noise? Was it really something or was Jeremiah's mind playing tricks on him. Jeremiah decided to try again.

"Is someone there?" Jeremiah called out.

Jeremiah heard a door opening. He tried to control himself, but the events he had been through had pushed him to the breaking point. Jeremiah began to sob.

"For the love of God man, either shoot me or let me go to the bathroom!" Jeremiah screamed. He decided mentally he had enough. Something had to give. If they were going to kill him so be it.

Jeremiah heard the door in front of him open very slowly. Sweat was pouring out of every pore of Jeremiah's body. He was sure he was about to die. Jeremiah realized he was wrong. He didn't want to die. Jeremiah was desperate.

"If you kill me," Jeremiah began. "You should know that my good friend, Agent John Fowler, will hunt you down."

Jeremiah listened and didn't hear anything. He panicked.

"Please don't kill me," Jeremiah sobbed. "I want to live." Jeremiah was crying freely. "I want to live."

1 Hour Earlier
John and Bruce Racing to Jeremiah's Location

Chapter 62

John's car topped out over 100 mph. Bruce had met him downstairs at the hotel and they had taken off. John glanced at Bruce's face for just a split second. He didn't dare look too long at the speeds he was driving.

What John saw, or didn't see, puzzled him. There was no emotion on Bruce's face. John played back through his head what Trip had said to John about Bruce back in the New York office. Could Bruce be a sociopath? If he was . . . John didn't like what was going through his mind. Bruce interrupted his thoughts.

"Is Trip okay? To lose someone like that must be absolutely tragic." Bruce said. John had filled in Bruce as to what had happened to Thelma.

"I don't know," John answered truthfully. "He's so wrapped up with your Dad right now that I don't know if he's allowing himself to process what has happened."

Bruce sat quietly for a second.

"If my father died, John," Bruce began. He didn't complete the sentence. John glanced at Bruce. He could see the sorrow on Bruce's face. He could see the worry. John silently chastised himself for thinking Bruce had been connected to Thelma or Sam.

"Bruce," John began. "How about you and I try to act like real human beings and put this rivalry behind us? I mean it's really gotten out of hand."

Bruce made a laughing noise in his throat. He smiled and nodded, never looking in John's direction.

Bruce was secretly celebrating inside. He had gotten John to feel sorry for him. If only he knew . . .

"I think that is an excellent idea, John," Bruce replied.

John started to say something but the GPS interrupted them. John navigated his way through the city streets to arrive at their destination. John looked around, thinking SWAT would already be at the scene. He picked up his phone to call Jessica to see where they were, when he noticed Bruce checking his gun. Bruce nodded at John and opened the car door. Bruce got out and headed toward the warehouse. John quickly opened his door and ran after Bruce.

Chapter 63

John finally caught up with Bruce inside the large warehouse. It was going to take some time to clear.

"Bruce," John hissed. "What are you doing?"

"My father is in there, John," Bruce replied in the same whispered tone. "What would you do if it was your Dad? Would you wait for backup?"

John nodded, frustrated. He knew exactly what he would do. They were going to have to do this alone.

"Ok," John relented. "But we do this slowly, clearing each room before we enter the next one."

Bruce nodded. They began to work their way through the warehouse, checking each room thoroughly before moving to the next one. Suddenly John grabbed Bruce's arm, stopping him. Bruce imagined pulling out a machete and chopping John's arm off for dare touching him, but he pushed the thought from his mind.

"Did you hear that?" John asked. Bruce hadn't heard anything. He listened carefully. There, he heard it. It sounded like someone shouting. They headed forward, carefully, but quickly. They heard noises from the door in front of them, and Bruce slowly opened the door. It creaked loudly. They heard a voice from inside.

"If you kill me," Jeremiah began. "You should know that my good friend, Agent John Fowler, will hunt you down."

John slowly closed his eyes. He knew Bruce was going to be livid over that one. He opened his eyes to see Bruce staring right at him.

"Well, at least his hero is here to save him," Bruce said. He gestured for John to go through the door first. John shook his head no. Bruce walked through the door as John heard the senator.

"Please don't kill me," Jeremiah sobbed. "I want to live." Jeremiah was crying freely. "I want to live."

Chapter 64

"Dad," Bruce called out. "It's me. Is anyone else here?"

"Bruce? Bruce, is that really you?" The Senator couldn't believe his ears. "No, Son. No, I don't think anyone else is here."

Bruce rushed over to his dad and started to untie him. John kept them covered. He reached for his cell phone and called Jessica.

"Jessica," John said. "We found him. Send an ambulance, but he looks okay."

John quickly hung up. The senator was hugging Bruce, and Bruce was looking very uncomfortable. The senator broke the hug and began to hurry across the room.

"Senator?" John asked. "Senator, where are you going?"

The senator never broke stride.

"John, good to see you, ole boy," the senator answered. "I have to go visit the water closet for a few moments. I do hope you'll excuse me."

As the senator closed the door to the bathroom, John looked at Bruce. John was softly chuckling. Bruce was looking at the bathroom door, shaking his head. As they were standing there, they heard loud noises coming from the rooms outside. They both crouched and aimed their guns at the open doorway. They both heard the unmistakable shout of Jessica.

"FBI!" She yelled.

"We're in here, Jessica, it's just us," replied John. Agents began to swarm the room, securing it. Trip and Jessica walked in, and looked around, confused.

"Bruce, John . . ." Trip began. "Where's the senator?"

John looked over at Bruce. Bruce extended his arm toward John as if to say, go ahead.

"Well, m'boy," John said in his best imitation of the Senator. "I say, the good senator had to visit the water closet and asked us if we would extend his regrets in missing you."

"That's good, John," Bruce said. "You should have worked an, 'I declare' in there somewhere, but that's good."

Jessica began to chuckle. Trip looked from Bruce to John and back. Trip looked at the ground and shook his head. At this moment the senator opened the bathroom door.

"Did I miss something?" The Senator asked.

"Not a thing, Dad," Bruce replied walking away. "Not a thing."

Chapter 65

Paramedics arrived at the warehouse along with FBI techs. The techs began to slowly process the entire scene. John, sitting on a desk, watched them from a distance. Right now he was really enjoying the war of words taking place between the senator and the EMTS. The EMTs were insisting Jeremiah go to the hospital. Jeremiah was insisting that he was fine. John was a little surprised when Bruce walked up and sat down beside him.

"Is there any chance of him actually going to the hospital?" John asked.

Bruce shook his head. He leaned forward and gripped the side of the desk with his hands.

"Actually, I think he will," Bruce replied. "This one scared him. I think he knows how close he came to dying and it's taken something out of him." John looked a bit surprised and then slowly nodded. Bruce turned toward John. "Thank you, John. You've found my father. You don't know what that means to me. There are things the senator needs to know that I've never had the courage to tell him. When all of this settles down, he and I are going to have a long talk."

Bruce was very proud of himself. He had told John the truth . . . he just hadn't told John what he and the senator would be talking about. John smiled and clapped Bruce on the shoulder. Bruce saw himself grabbing John's arm and twisting it out of the socket. Bruce pushed the mental image aside. John removed his hand from Bruce's shoulder and looked back over at the EMTs continuing to argue with the senator. John shook his head, smiled, and looked back at Bruce.

"We're not done yet you know," John replied. "We need to talk to him, and soon, Bruce."

"I know we do, but we both know who was behind the kidnapping," Bruce stated. "That little weasel Luke did it for the former First Lady's affections."

"That may be true, Bruce, but we have to prove it first," John said. "I would love to hear that Archibald had something to do with it."

John slid off the desk. His cell phone buzzed and John looked down at it. He had just received a text from an unknown number. David George, the man who had tried to kill the former First Lady, had texted him.

"John, it's David George. I just wanted to let you know that I have agreed to go into a psychiatric hospital. Charges are not going to be pressed against me. Please find something on the Staples family soon. I don't know if I can handle the nightmares they cause me. I keep having dreams of getting my own brand of justice, and I need to have peace."

John showed Bruce the text. Bruce whistled.

"John," Bruce said. "That guy may be a special kind of crazy. He isn't done with them yet."

"I know," John replied. "I hope they keep him locked up for a while. I'm not convinced he won't try to kill Veronica or Archibald."

"Would that be a bad thing?" Bruce asked.

John shot Bruce a look and Bruce smiled broadly. John shook his head and chuckled. He looked down at the text again and re-read it. John had a sinking feeling that things were getting worse instead of better.

**David George
Psychiatric Hospital**

Chapter 66

Tom Evans, David George's lawyer, looked quite
upset. That was nothing new for Tom. He was always
upset. He couldn't understand why he kept getting clients
that wouldn't listen to his legal advice. Tom had just sent
Special Agent John Fowler a text. It was from his current
client, against Tom's advice. Tom normally wouldn't do
something like that, but David didn't have access to a cell
phone, and Tom had learned that David could be quite
persuasive when he wanted to be. Quite honestly, David
scared Tom.

Tom didn't like David George. In fact, Tom was
certain David had murdered five people and would have
killed the First Lady if it hadn't been for Agent Fowler.

"Something wrong, Tom?" David asked, jerking
Tom away from his thoughts.

"Yes," Tom replied forcefully, but nervously. "You
don't listen to any of the advice I have given you. You
don't like me." David smiled and shrugged his shoulders.
Tom ignored him and continued. "Why do you keep me
on?"

"A buddy said you were the best," David replied.
"It's not your job to judge me Tom; it's your job to keep me
out of prison."

"You're a very evil man," Tom spat.

David's eyes grew very small. His nostrils began to
flare, and a reddish hue came over his skin. Tom gulped.
He knew he had just crossed a line. David spoke very
quietly.

"I'm evil?" David asked. "I'm evil? Tom, you haven't witnessed evil until you meet Veronica Staples. That girl killed my sister for nothing. My sister shared her greatest secret with Veronica, and she killed her. Then, to top it off she tried to have me killed. Why? Because she was afraid of what it would do to her image! I'm evil? I'm evil!" David's voice had been getting louder throughout the conversation. Tom was very nervous. He was afraid David was about to lash out. David realized what was going on, and calmed down. David smiled at Tom.

"Sorry, Tom," David said. Tom was still scared. David leaned forward and whispered to Tom. "I'm going to let you in on a little secret. I'm going to give Agent Fowler a chance to take care of the Staples, and if he doesn't, then I'm going to . . . permanently."

David leaned back in his chair and began to chuckle. The chuckle continued to get louder and louder until he was in a full laughing fit. Tom was terrified. He was convinced David was crazy. As soon as David was admitted, Tom fled the hospital and promised himself that he would send David a letter letting him know he was dropping David as a client. Tom thought he might move as well, just in case David ever got out and came looking for him.

John Fowler
Warehouse in Baltimore, Maryland

Chapter 67

John watched as they loaded the senator into the ambulance. He had really wanted to question Jeremiah, and so had Jessica. He had to remind Jessica that the senator was not a suspect. Jessica didn't find that comment very funny. Bruce climbed into the ambulance with his father. John never thought he would see the day where those two got along. It was quite sad it took a near death experience to do it. John turned and saw Jessica, Chet, and Trip watching him. John pressed his lips together and blew air into his cheeks, looking like a chipmunk. He knew he had to go talk to his friends.

As he walked toward them, John thought back to a conversation he and Sam had once had. She had wanted him to attend a ball hosted by her parents. John had completely resisted, but had finally relented when he had learned that Senator Cosby was going to attend. John smiled. It had been the Senator's idea for the three of them to team up together. From that point on, well, as they say, the rest was history. He looked at the group and realized that there was a new history, one that he wasn't part of. John realized he was feeling regret. Regret for the years he had walked away on the people that had tried to help him. John stopped in front of the group, trying to figure out what to say.

"You okay?" Trip asked John.

"Not hardly," John replied. "See, I've got this thing you all know about, but what you don't realize is I just assume everyone thinks the same way I do, and, well, that never ends well. What I'm fumbling around with Trip, is

I'm sorry. I made that crime scene about me, I made Thelma's death about Sam, and frankly I acted like it was all about me. I'm sorry."

Trip was quiet for a minute. Jessica stomped on Trip's foot.

"What!" Trip exclaimed. Jessica motioned toward John. John was chuckling.

"It's okay, Trip," John said. "I get it. If I was you I'd relish this moment as well. We both know that it's not often that I apologize."

"And that moment's over," Chet deadpanned. The group began to laugh. Trip put out his hand with a broad smile on his face, and John shook it. John couldn't remember the last time he had this many people around him that he had felt comfortable with. Maybe I'm growing up, John thought . . . Nah.

Chapter 68

A tech, looking extremely nervous, approached the group of four.

"Director Smothers?" The tech asked.

"Right here, Son," Trip responded. The tech handed Trip a document. John's eyebrow went up.

"Is that what I think it is, Trip?" John asked.

"If you mean a warrant to search Archibald Staples home, you would be correct," Trip replied. John was stunned.

"How did you pull that off?" John asked.

"After you left to pick up Bruce, I called in a favor with a judge. I laid out the facts; the senator was thought to be in a building in a shell corporation in his daughter's name," Trip replied. "Veronica is now living with daddy dearest. The judge said if we find the senator or proof that he was there he would sign off on the warrant. Once we found the senator I called him back. The judge wasn't crazy about it, but he eventually signed off."

John was smiling broadly. Trip got very serious.

"Look you three; this is our best chance to bust this guy," Trip said. "Go in there and do what you do best, but do it by the book. This weasel has slipped out of every trap that has been set for him. I want him. I want him locked up for the rest of his pitiful life."

John was staring Trip right in the eye.

"Any chance that warrant covers phones?" John asked, his mind already turning. He was thinking about finding some link between Archibald and the killer.

Trip smiled broadly, thinking the same way John was. "It does, John, but you and I both know he probably used a burn phone if he ordered any deaths."

Jessica stepped between the two of them. "Gentlemen, we're looking for anything to do with the senator's kidnapping," she said. "We have no proof on

Archibald having anything to do with anyone's death. Are we clear?"

John and Trip both nodded. John glanced at Chet. John knew there was no way Chet could go to Archibald's given what he uncovered. John glanced back at Trip. Trip was having the same thoughts. He thought for a second, and nodded. He started to stay something, but John held up his hand. Trip nodded, but Chet cut both of them off.

"Director Smothers, I would like to be recused of this case," Chet said.

"I thought only judges could recuse themselves," John said. Jessica stomped on his foot, never taking her eyes off of Chet. John hopped in place. Trip rolled his eyes at John. John tried to look sheepish as he hopped. Trip turned back to Chet.

"Trip, I can't be on this case," Chet said. "We all know what might come out if I was. I don't care about me, but it could cost you your job."

Trip nodded. He turned toward Jessica and John.

"If you two can behave for 5 minutes, I want you, along with 50 or so agents to execute this search warrant. In fact, I want the 50 or so agents to execute the warrant and you to watch Archibald. I want you to get any clue you can off of that man!"

John smiled and saluted. Jessica grabbed his arm and dragged him away before Trip strangled him.

"What is wrong with you?" Jessica asked.

"I just enjoy irritating Trip," John replied.

"Well, you're irritating more than just him," Jessica replied.

"Pfffbbtt," John replied. "Don't worry about Chet, he's used to me."

Jessica opened the car door and looked over at John.

"For someone so good at picking up clues, you miss the obvious," Jessica said. "That was strike two." Jessica got in the driver's side leaving John standing with the door opened. He was confused.

"You're getting irritated with me?" John asked.

"Getting implies I'm not there yet, and that would be a wrong assumption," Jessica said very quietly.

John got in the passenger side and looked over at Jessica.

You do realize you're driving my in-laws car, right?" John asked. Jessica ignored him, started the car and drove off. John didn't say anything for several miles down the road. When he spoke it was quietly and somberly.

"Are you breaking up with me?" John asked.

"What?" Jessica exclaimed, almost wrecking the car. She looked at him for a moment and realized he was being very serious.

"John, was Sam your only girlfriend? I mean are you telling me you didn't have one in middle school, high school or college. I just assumed you meant she was the only serious girlfriend you ever had. Are you saying she was the only one . . . ever?" Jessica asked. John sucked in one side of his jaw and stared straight ahead at the road.

"Is that a trick question?" John asked.

"How could that be a trick question?" Jessica asked.

"Is it a trick question?" John asked. He looked at Jessica. Jessica was very confused. "I guess I only have . . . " John stopped and then started again. "I guess it depends on how you define . . . " He stopped again. He swallowed and spoke quietly. "I mean are you . . . do you consider yourself . . . " John looked down at the floorboard.

"I would be your second girlfriend in your entire life if I was?" Jessica asked.

John slowly nodded his head. Jessica didn't know what to say. She thought for a moment. She reached over and took John's hand.

"We're not breaking up, John," Jessica said quietly.

Rosa Martinez
Staples Home, Virginia

Chapter 69

Rosa Martinez hated her job. She had worked for the Staples for 10 years. During that time Archibald believed she was an illegal alien and that she didn't understand English. Rosa had tried to talk to Archibald many times when she was first employed but the only thing Archibald would ever say to her was, "No hablo espanol."

Rosa had heard things over the years that sickened her. Archibald would always talk about his deals and plans in front of her. If anyone said anything about Rosa, Archibald would say things like, "She doesn't understand," or "She's not from around these parts," and laugh about it. Everyone talked in front of Rosa like she didn't exist. Rosa hated the way it made her feel.

Rosa realized over time if Archibald ever found out she could speak and understand English she would be killed. It was that simple. Archibald was a dangerous man. She had told herself many times she would quit over the years, but Archibald paid her such a good wage she didn't know if she could. Plus she worried if she did try to quit, Archibald would have her killed.

Today was worse than usual. Her best friend, Thelma had been murdered last night. Rosa and Thelma had been paintball enthusiasts. They played in Dale City, where Thelma lived. Rosa never told Thelma who she worked for. She knew if she did Thelma would try to get Rosa out from under Archibald's influence, but Rosa worried for Thelma's life.

Rosa felt awful. Thelma had talked to her last night about her friend from New York. Rosa knew Thelma was in love with him, even if Thelma would never admit it. Thelma had told her that he was working on a big case and she was doing him a favor. Rosa smiled at the memory. The only time Thelma had ever not wanted to play laser tag with Rosa was when Thelma's special man was in town.

If all of this wasn't bad enough, "The Princess" as the staff referred to her, had returned. Rosa wasn't sure which was worse, the mood Archibald had been in when he thought Veronica's life was in danger, or the mood he had been in since she had been arrested. Rosa just wanted to finish her work and go home for the day. As luck would have it, it was this moment and place that Veronica chose to confront Archibald in front of Rosa.

Chapter 70

Archibald was at his desk going through reports. Rosa was quickly, and quietly, cleaning. Archibald watched her for a moment. Something seemed to be bothering her. Archibald shook his head in disgust. There were days he thought about getting rid of her, but Duck had told him she was worthless to him. Archibald thought about having it taken care of the old fashioned way, but decided against it. There were too many eyes on Veronica right now. The last thing he needed was an investigation over an illegal. His thoughts were interrupted by Veronica bursting in the room. She was holding a newspaper.

"I know you had something to do with this!" Veronica exclaimed. "Are you getting senile, or just old?"

Archibald groaned inwardly. He knew Veronica would be impossible to live with for a while. In a few days she had gone from being what she thought was the most powerful woman in the US, if not the world, to having to move back in with Daddy. Archibald chuckled at that thought. Millions of people would give anything to move into this mansion. Veronica was waving a hand in front of his face.

"Hello," she called sarcastically. "Is there anyone home in there?"

"Lisa, dear, or is it Veronica again?" Archibald asked. Veronica looked irritated for just a moment, and then she laughed.

"Do you really think it bothers me?" She asked. "Do you think I care what those fatcats in Washington think?" She walked over to the window in the office and looked outside. "I think I will go back to Veronica. The world knows how I was attacked, so there's no need for secrecy any longer." Archibald loved how she had practiced the lie of how she was attacked so many times over the years she kept up the appearance even with the one

160

person that knew the truth. She turned back toward her father, pointing at the lead story. It was the death of Thelma. Rosa could see it clearly from her position in the room.

"Did you do this, Dad?" Veronica asked. "Did you have this woman killed? Are you stupid enough to do that, Dad?"

Rosa held her breath as she waited for the answer.

Chapter 71

"Veronica, you'd better sit down," Archibald said.

"Oh, Dad," Veronica began. She sat in the chair. "What stupid thing did you do?"

"I tell you what I didn't do," Archibald said, appearing to be getting angrier by the second. "I didn't lead on some fool Secret Service agent until he thought up the crazy scheme of kidnapping one of the most powerful politicians in the world!"

Veronica was sitting in the chair across from her father, with her right elbow on the arm of the chair. Her thumb was under her chin with her index finger over her upper lip. When she heard her father, instead of getting angry, a slow grin began to cross her face. She began to lightly chuckle. She was quite proud of herself.

"I did do that didn't I?" she asked. "But he got you to go along with it." The anger left Archibald's face. He leaned back in his chair and began to chuckle as well.

"You did, and well done may I add," Archibald said approvingly.

"What a dope," Veronica said, referring to Luke.

"He was, but it's time we talked about some steps I had to take to ensure your safety after you were arrested," Archibald said. "I did what Luke couldn't and reached out to Bruce Cosby, the FBI agent. That boy does not seem to like his father."

Veronica smiled at the last statement her father made. Rosa continued cleaning, while listening intently. She was being ignored as usual, but she made sure neither of the Staples realized what she was doing.

Archibald paused for a second. He was internally debating how much to tell Veronica, but he knew she would harass him if he didn't. Besides, she knew so much on him that the death of an FBI employee was actually quite small on the list of his transgressions.

"Bruce and I set-up your boy toy to be a fall guy," Archibald said. Veronica visibly winced at the term for Luke, but continued to smile wickedly. "The problem we ran into was John and his little troop."

Veronica scowled. "We may have to do something about them," she said. Archibald nodded in agreement.

"Apparently someone got wise to Bruce, so I had Duck's inside man to intercept some evidence John's group was trying to collect on Bruce. I informed Bruce of the situation, and Bruce actually took care of the person in the paper, but he was very unhappy to hear about the inside man."

Rosa's heart leapt in her throat with that revelation. Her friend had been killed by an FBI agent. Rosa had to fight back tears. She couldn't let the two of them find her out now. She promised herself that she would tell someone what had happened. In fact, she needed to find the agent Thelma always talked about being the best in the FBI. She needed to find John Fowler.

Chapter 72

"Wouldn't Bruce be surprised to learn there's more than one inside?" Veronica asked. Rosa nearly fell over hearing that. Archibald squirmed uncomfortably in his seat.

"Well," Archibald began. "I had to let that fish off the hook."

"What!" Veronica exclaimed. "Why?"

"Settle down," Archibald said. "You know that piece of land I've been trying to get out of the Moores?" Veronica nodded. "Arthur agreed to sell it on two conditions. One, he bought out the FBI agents marker. The second condition was he bought the private student loans off of me."

Veronica took a second to process the information. She nodded as she thought. She looked sharply at her father.

"They know?" She simply asked. Archibald looked slightly annoyed.

"They suspect," he replied. "If they knew, there would be a thousand agents swarming this house. They suspect small things; they don't know the big things."

Veronica sat in the chair with her elbows on the arms, and her fingers drumming together in front of her face. Archibald watched her for a second.

"The most they suspect me for is covering up that George girl's death," Archibald said. "They have tried for years to bring me down. We're untouchable, Veronica. Don't worry. Besides, I'm quite sure Bruce is going to clean up any lingering mess." Archibald smiled as he reached for his drink; he paused right as the drink reached his mouth. "That boy does have a voracious appetite for violence."

Veronica stopped drumming her fingers together with that last statement. She looked at her father suspiciously. A slow grin crossed her face.

"You've used him before." It wasn't a question, but a statement. A large grin came over Archibald's face. He finished his drink, and then wiped his mouth with his sleeve. An evil grin covered his face.

"Well," he wavered, smiling the entire time.

"Tell me," Veronica said. Archibald looked toward the ceiling, thinking back. He looked at Veronica and smiled broadly.

"Do you remember when the Senator was making serious noise about running for President against your," Archibald paused. Veronica tried to look putout about what her father was dancing around, but she didn't really care about her ex-husband. Well, he wasn't her ex-husband yet, but in her mind he might as well be.

"Let's say former husband," Archibald said. Veronica nodded. "I had been wondering what would stop Jeremiah from running, but not be directly traced to me, and then everything just fell in my lap."

Chapter 73

Veronica was leaning forward in her seat, intrigued with what she was hearing. Rosa couldn't believe her ears. Archibald continued.

"I was at an event and ran into Bruce," Archibald said. "He had just been upstaged again by John Fowler, and would have been watching John and his father having their picture taken together . . . again, if John had been there and hadn't been working undercover." Archibald paused for a second. "You know, you have to be impressed with the FBI. They made it believable John had been drummed out of the FBI. Duck was smart though, he didn't buy it. He didn't think that a girl like Samantha Moore would have stayed with a drunk, on the take, former FBI agent. Duck was smart enough to jump on the leftovers though, wasn't he?" Archibald's eyes twinkled. He was very proud of what he and Duck had pulled off those years ago. Archibald pulled himself back into the present and continued the story.

"Where was I?" Archibald asked to no one in particular. "Oh yes, Bruce was looking extremely upset, and I decided to see what I could do to stir the pot. I was trying to make small talk with Bruce, and I jokingly asked him about his father." Archibald lit a cigar and began to smoke it. He was clearly enjoying the memory. "I told him it looked like his father was on the way to being president. I said the only thing that would keep it from happening was some skeleton in the closet. I paused, and jokingly asked Bruce if his father had anything in the closet that the press might dig up. Bruce looked even more upset than before and stormed off. I had no idea what button I had pushed, but I was enjoying myself.

"Well, what I asked Bruce clearly bothered him. He asked me about it again later in the evening. He wanted to know if it was true. I asked him what he was talking about, and he pointblank asked me if the rumors of his father and the Moore lady were true.

"I was stunned by the question. I asked him what had brought that up. He told me an interested party had asked him, 'Don't you find it odd that Sam has the exact same color eyes as your father and not the color of her parents.' I didn't say anything, but just smiled. I wanted to work this for all it was worth, anything to mess with Jeremiah. Bruce left me for a bit. When he came back, he was visibly shaken."

"Dad," Veronica began. "Are you telling me that fool believed that the most disgustingly decent man I have ever seen in my life had an affair?" Archibald didn't answer. He smiled broadly at Veronica, got up, and refilled his drink.

"If John Fowler ever found out," she began. Archibald cut her off. He was waving his hand holding his drink.

"How?" Archibald asked. "And so what if he did? I never told Bruce to kill her. I never told Bruce anything. I just let his crazy mind jump to all sorts of conclusions."

"You know for a fact that he killed her?" Veronica asked. Archibald smiled evilly again.

"We had that conversation a week before her death," Archibald said. "At her funeral, Bruce came up to me and asked the conversation we had stay between us. I agreed, of course. He then informed me his father was going to pull out of the primary race. Sam's death and John's reaction had been too much for Senator Cosby. So, my dear, I didn't have to worry about Cosby getting too much power and you got to become First Lady, and I truly didn't have to do a thing"

Veronica's face fell with that last statement. Archibald noticed and started to apologize when Veronica waved him off.

"That was the other thing I wanted to tell you, Dad," Veronica began. "I just got a text before I came in here to talk to you. Apparently after my husband resigns, the current Vice-President is set to nominate Jeremiah Cosby as the new Vice-President."

Archibald swallowed the drink in his hand. He then threw the glass against the wall causing it to explode. Rosa knew to yell out in Spanish. Archibald stormed from the room. Veronica followed after him, yelling at Rosa to clean up the mess. Rosa began to clean up the glass fragments. She needed to find John Fowler, quickly.

Jessica and John
On the way to the Staples

Chapter 74

As John and Jessica were heading toward the Staple mansion, John's and Jessica's cell phones both went off. John checked his phone and saw a text from Trip about Jeremiah being recommended as Vice-President. Jessica handed John her phone and he saw Trip had sent her the same message.

"Trip sent us the same message," John said. "Jeremiah is about to be recommended to be the next Vice-President when the current Vice-President takes over the office."

"You're about to have a very powerful friend in a very powerful position, John," Jessica replied. John shrugged.

"Are you okay to drive?" John asked. "I mean I know you had a late night with me two nights ago, and you didn't have any sleep last night due to Thelma and Archibald."

Jessica smiled at John, "I'm good, John," she replied. "Besides, there is no way I would pass up driving this car. Anyway, I'm the younger one of the two of us."

"You act as if I'm ancient," John replied.

"Why don't you try and find something on the radio," Jessica said, trying to change the subject. John started playing with the radio dial. He looked at his watch and started trying to find a sports channel.

"What are you looking for?" Jessica asked with a smirk on her face. John saw the smirk and was a little annoyed.

"A radio station, if that's okay," John replied a little testily.

"You know you can have scores sent right to your phone," Jessica said, still smirking. John stared at his phone for a second. He looked at Jessica and then back at the phone.

"You could just ask me, you know," Jessica said coyly. John looked at her questioningly.

"Ask you what?" John said. Jessica sighed and rolled her eyes.

"If they won last night. You do remember I am a FBI agent as well?" Jessica asked. John feigned ignorance. "Oh, for crying out loud, John! It's March, you're an avid college basketball fan, and the Cats played last night." Jessica looked at John, who was more than a little impressed.

"Sam told you, didn't she?" John asked. Jessica sighed loudly.

"John," she began. "You know I have worked with you for a long time. The only websites you know how to access are sports. You constantly go on about the differences between a 2-3 zone and man to man defense. You go on and on about how you prefer the college three point line be at 19 feet 9 inches. And finally, you're from Kentucky where you go on and on about college basketball being king."

John sat there quietly for a moment. He was smiling.

"I forget how you can get wound up without any sleep," John said. Jessica made a face and waved him off. "Jessica, I'm sorry about earlier. I haven't been around actual people for the most part in the last three years. I've only had one romance in my life, and I don't want to go back to what I was."

Jessica glanced over at John. He was looking at the floorboard. She knew she should let him off easy, but their relationship has been built on them going back and forth since they became partners. She wasn't going to let their new relationship change that.

"First off, you're forgiven about how you were acting. We're all a little on edge, and very sleep deprived, and quite frankly you're learning how to coexist with human beings again." John chuckled and looked over at Jessica. She looked quite serious. The smile fell from John's face and he tried to appear serious as well.

"As for the other," she continued. "It doesn't bother me that you don't have a lot of experience with women."

"Hey! I have plenty of experience!" John exclaimed.

"What bothers me is you're just like all typical men," she went on, ignoring him. "You talk a big game and when it comes to game time you all fall short."

"Now wait just a minute!" John retorted.

"For just once in my life," Jessica plowed ahead. "I would like for a man to be upfront and honest about what they are looking for." She held up a finger before John could speak. John had never seen this side of Jessica before, but then again, he had never been in this situation with Jessica before. "I would like a man to understand it is my choice what I do or do not do and what I do or do not do does not make me a tease, or scared of a real man, or, my personal favorite," Jessica threw up air quotes. "'You know what would fix her?' What I agree to do or not do with my body is my choice, and not only do I expect to have that right, but I expect to be respected for it; whatever it is I decide to do."

"You know you covered a lot of ground there about a man being up front, and you being respected," John said.

"Well, I did get on a bit of a roll, but it's how I feel," Jessica replied.

"Let me ask you this," John said. Jessica nodded for him to go ahead. "If you expect for a man to be up front, shouldn't a man expect you to be up front with him?"

"That's reasonable," Jessica replied, nodding. John waited. Jessica glanced over at him and shrugged her shoulders. "Oh, so you expect me to be up front first?"

"Any reason why I shouldn't?" John asked.

"Ever heard of being a gentleman and going first?" Jessica asked.

"I'm a liberated man," John replied tugging on his jacket. Jessica sputtered laughter with that remark. She looked at him for a second and decided to be bold.

"So, you want to have sex with me?" Jessica asked.

Chapter 75

John's mother had always warned him to be careful what you asked because the answer you got may not be the one you wanted, or was ready for. John thought for a second very carefully. He glanced over at Jessica who didn't look the least bit nervous or embarrassed with what she had just asked him. John thought she could at least have the decency to look slightly uncomfortable.

"John," Jessica said quietly. "Big boys and girls can talk about these sorts of things now."

John nodded, and still was silent. It was time to put on his big boy pants.

"I don't think it's a question of me wanting to have sex with you," John responded. Jessica raised one eyebrow quizzically. "I don't know of any heterosexual male that wouldn't want to have sex with you. The question is when do I feel comfortable having sex with you and when do you feel comfortable having sex with me."

Jessica thought about John's answer for a moment. She began to worry that John's statement had a very deep meaning.

"Jess, this has nothing to do with Sam," John said. "This has to do with my feelings and what I believe and who I am."

"You don't want to have sex until you get married, do you, John?" Jessica asked. John looked down at the floorboard. "Answer me, John," Jessica said.

"No," John replied. "It's not you; it's just something I believe in. I know it's old fashioned and many guys would think I'm out of my mind, but no. It's not even necessarily religious. It's about commitment. I know I talk and make innuendos sometimes, but I believe there is only one for me, and I am going to honor that other person. I know that sounds very 1800s and Puritan, but it's what I believe. In case you wondering, I also realize this is my decision and I cannot hold anyone I choose to have a relationship with to my beliefs. What they did, or didn't do, before me is none of my concern. But if they're going to be in a relationship with me, then they're going to have to accept who I am." He paused and looked over at Jessica. He spoke very softly. "Is that a deal breaker?"

"Who says I would have sex with you or anyone else before I married?" Jessica asked. John grinned at her.

"Well . . . ?" John asked.

"John," Jessica began, smiling. "That's a very personal question. That's the kind of information I'd only share with someone I'm in a deep committed relationship with. I am in a relationship with you. I have no idea what kind it is at this moment, but I am committed to it. Is that enough?"

John thought for a minute.

"This relationship is going to get me committed one day," John said under his breath. Jessica heard him, and tried to fight back a smile. John glanced over and saw her fighting the smile, but decided to let it go.

"So basically you've managed to get me to tell you my entire past," John began.

"What there was of it," Jessica responded.

"Got me to admit my feelings for you and what type of relationship I want with any woman and you've told me . . . nothing?" John asked. Jessica nodded.

"You're the one who said it was none of your concern. Got a problem with that?" She asked curtly. John shook his head no. Jessica smiled.

"Let's, just for fun, say I did," John said cautiously.

"First, you'd be a hypocrite with that little speech you just gave. Second . . . . I'd tell you to get over it," Jessica said as she pulled into the Staples drive. "We've got a big bad to take down." Jessica stopped at the gate, leaned over to John, and kissed him. When she pulled back, she winked at him. "I'll say this, whenever we decide to do whatever, I promise you won't be sorry."

"I believe you," John replied breathlessly.

Chapter 76

John and Jessica were admitted to the house by one of Archibald's lackeys. As they approached the house, John looked back toward the road and saw a whole fleet of cars and vans headed toward the house. John smiled inwardly. Trip had said fifty agents would be joining them, and apparently he wasn't kidding. Jessica was serving the warrant to Archibald and one of his lawyers when John spotted the former First lady.

"Mrs. Nichols," John said, tipping his hat. He paused and looked at Archibald. Archibald looked very unhappy. "My apologies, ma'am, is that Staples now?"

"You may call me Veronica," Veronica replied, her voice dripping with honey. John smiled at her. Jessica shot John a look.

"Jessica," John began. "Have you met Veronica? You remember she's the lady I got Trip to arrest in the White House a few days ago."

Jessica smiled sweetly at Veronica. Veronica began to scowl and huffed off. Archibald roared with laughter.

"John," Archibald began, slapping him on the back as he led the two agents to the house. "I needed that."

"Hear some bad news there, Archibald?" John asked. "I'm sure by now you've heard the news about Senator Cosby." John stopped and faced Archibald. "Or is it that you had some investments bought off you, and the 'assets' that were in those packages won't be able to be used the way you thought they would?" Jessica had a scowl on her face as John said this. Archibald spread his hands.

"I'm quite sure I don't know what you're talking about, Agent Fowler," Archibald replied. He looked over at Jessica. "Miss Hammerstein, why the look on your face? You're much too beautiful to look like that. Come in, and feel free to search wherever you want and talk to whoever you want."

John smiled. "Whoever?" John asked. Archibald nodded. "Are you sure Archibald?"

"Be my guest," Archibald answered as he walked away from the agents. "Most of the housekeeping staff can't speak English." John was glancing around as Archibald was talking. He noticed one of Archibald's staff. A slow smile spread across his face. "Oh, and if you should find any of them to be illegal, please, deport them immediately," Archibald continued. "I do try and make sure they are legal, but you know how they can be."

"They!" Jessica exclaimed.

"Yes," Archibald replied. "Those illegals will do anything to take our hard earned American dollars. I honestly hate paying them, but they work so hard for so little." Jessica was boiling.

"You know," John began. "I thought Veronica was the biggest piece of slime I ever met. I was so wrong; she got all her evil honestly. Archibald, I swear to you if it's the last thing I do I'm going to bring you down." Archibald drew up and had a look of pure hate on his face. John leaned in real close. "It's a shame Veronica's ex-husband won the presidency, because if it had been Jeremiah, I would have been your permanent shadow until we stuff you and your pompous daughter in jail." John waited for Archibald to respond, but he didn't. Archibald just turned and left the room. Jessica looked at John, smiled, and nodded.

"I noticed you looking around when Archibald was talking," Jessica said. "I also saw that famous John grin." That statement caused John to smile. Jessica stepped very close. "What did I miss?" She asked.

John leaned forward and whispered into Jessica's ear where only she could hear.

"You mean besides the fact that I'm the man of your dreams?" John asked. Jessica rolled her eyes.

"Archibald's housekeeper can speak English, and I think from the way she's acting, she knows something." Jessica's eyes went wide, and John leaned back, grinning like a Cheshire cat.

Chapter 77

"How in the world can you possibly think that?" Jessica asked. She kept glancing at the housekeeper that John had pointed out to her. John grabbed Jessica by the shoulder and walked her outside as the FBI techs began to file into the house and process it.

"Keep your voice down," John whispered. "I don't think Archibald knows. Her body is reacting to everything Archibald is saying, if she doesn't understand English, how is that possible? We need to get her out of here. If she does understand English, there is no telling what that egotistical nut said in front of her and what he would do if he figured it out."

Jessica nodded. "Let me handle this," she whispered. She walked through the door and John followed her. She walked up toward the housekeeper. John noticed the housekeeper watching Jessica. John made eye contact with the housekeeper, and winked at her. For a spit second fear covered Rosa's face and then she saw John's smile. Relief began to spread across her face.

"FBI," Jessica said loudly to Rosa. Jessica pulled out her badge and put it close to Rosa's face where she could see it. "Ma'am I have to take you in for questioning." Archibald came around the corner and saw what was going on. John waved at Archibald and smiled. Archibald waved them off and went back to his office. Rosa went quietly with Jessica. She stopped in front of two agents, Jeff and Steve, which were searching the premises.

"Do you two think you can handle this search?" Jessica asked. The two nodded. "Remember, guys, this has to be by the book." They nodded again. They didn't notice John behind them. As Jessica walked away, John leaned in between them.

"Just so you know, I read Agent Hammerstein's report, she covered you two," John said. The two agents smiled. "If it had been me, I'd of hung the both of you out to dry. Just so you know." John walked off as the two agents stood there dumbfounded. John got in the car after Jessica and Rosa. The car took off toward the road.

"Please, you have to let me talk to Agent John Fowler," Rosa pleaded.

Jessica looked over at John. John nodded slowly.

"You know for someone who supposedly can't speak English you do a great job of it," John stated. Rosa sighed.

"That idiot," Rosa said. John and Jessica laughed out loud. Rosa was a little taken aback, but she continued. "He thinks anyone that has a Spanish or Mexican sounding name can't speak English. I was born in the US for crying out loud. Please you must let me talk to John Fowler."

"You know," John began. "There are days I even impress myself. I have never met you before in my life, ma'am." John reached out his hand. "My name is John Fowler." Rosa shook John's hand eagerly.

"I have to talk to you about my good friend Thelma," Rosa began. "An FBI agent named Bruce killed her."

"Jessica," John said not taking his eyes of Rosa. "Let's get to the Moores pronto. I'll have Trip meet us there." Jessica nodded and floored the accelerator.

Jeff and Steve
Inside Archibald's Mansion

Chapter 77

Jeff and Steve were conducting the sweep of
Archibald's mansion, but both of them were burning up
inside from what John had said to them. Archibald had
noticed when John and Jessica had taken away Rosa that
words had been exchanged between the two hot shot agents
and the two men. Archibald was happy to finally be rid of
the housekeeper He had no idea what her name was.
Archibald had one of his lawyers snap pictures of the two
men. The lawyer came back with the pictures, and
Archibald had the lawyer forward the pictures to a cell
phone number. A few minutes later Archibald's cell phone
rang.

"Hello," Archibald answered.

"Quack," the man on the other end answered.
Archibald laughed. It was Duck. Duck had spread terror
through the underworld during his rise to power, but he
also understood that he had an odd moniker. He used it to
his advantage. He had the ability of identifying himself
without ever saying his name. Any fool could say quack
into a phone, and no one could prove it actually was Robert
Duck Mariotti Jr, the alleged head of a Mafia family.

"They're perfect," Duck said. "2 cents each in
student loans." With that the line went dead. Archibald
smiled and nodded at his lawyer, who hurried out of the
room. Centomila in Italian meant one hundred thousand.
Duck was telling Archibald that each agent owed over two
hundred thousand dollars in student loans. Archibald
handed his phone to his most trusted security man and

walked out of the room. The security man began to destroy the phone.

Archibald turned, went out of the office and headed outside. After a few minutes the lawyer who had taken the pictures walked up to him. The lawyer pulled out the financials for both agents. Approximately 55 thousand dollars of both men's loans were in the hands of the federal government. The other 145 thousand were in the hands of private companies, most of which Archibald owned. The lawyer showed Archibald that the two men owed over 120 thousand between them to companies owned by Archibald. Archibald handed the sheet back to the lawyer who immediately put it in his briefcase.

Archibald knew he was being bold, but he knew anything that was even remotely incriminating was in the hands of his lawyers, and Archibald was ready to use attorney/client privilege. He wasn't 100% sure that would protect him from everything, but Archibald was certain these FBI agents wouldn't know for sure either. Archibald had gotten away with so much for so long that he was ready for a challenge, and the only way that would happen was for him to give them something. They wouldn't win. Archibald always won, sometimes he had to cheat to win, but in the end he always won.

Chapter 78

Archibald walked up to the two men who had been left in charge of the investigation. He stood between the two and stared straight ahead.

"It's a shame, you know," Archibald said. He lit a cigar and took a few puffs. "He's put you two to work to get his glory, and when he doesn't find anything, he's going to have you two fired."

The agents didn't say anything, but they exchanged a quick glance. Archibald continued to talk.

"I'm not the bad man everyone thinks I am. My daughter had something horrible happen to her, when she was attacked by that girl years ago. Yes I helped her change her identity. If I made a mistake it was because I was trying to be a good father. I won't apologize for that. I have made a serious mistake, and I would like to rectify it, but I would like to avoid any undo arrests."

The two agents looked at each other. Jeff nodded to Steve. Steve spoke.

"We're listening, Mr. Staples."

Archibald laughed and held out his hand to Steve.

"Steve McIntosh, I believe," Archibald said as he shook Steve's hand. Archibald turned to Jeff. "Jeff Hart?" Jeff nodded. "Men, Luke called me a few days ago about some outrageous plan to protect my daughter. I thought he had been working too many hours and ignored it. I didn't want to destroy a man's career in the Secret Service." The two agents nodded. Archibald continued.

"Then my daughter gets taken hostage, and arrested. I never thought once about the senator. I didn't." The two agents nodded, sympathetically. Archibald was loving it. He was drawing them in. "Then my daughter gets home and tells me about the Secret Service agent that has fallen in love with her." Archibald paused and shook his head. One of the agents put his hand comfortingly on Archibald's shoulder. Archibald knew he had them. "I have a tape of him that I need to give to you."

The agents thought they had struck it rich. Steve looked at Jeff, and Jeff nodded.

"Mr. Staples," Jeff began. "If there is something that you have that will help us close this case, we can help make sure you are protected. We're not interested in hurting an innocent man. Let's face it, your family has taken a beating in the media the past few days. I'm sure your lawyer has advised you to hand over the tape and we can work out any silly misunderstandings." All three men looked over at Archibald's lawyer. The lawyer nodded once. Archibald looked back at the agents and sighed. He put his hands in his pockets and looked down at the floor. The entire time all Archibald could think of was how he duped the FBI, yet again. After a minute or so of this, Archibald finally nodded at his lawyer. The lawyer reached into his briefcase and produced a tape and a tape recorder. Archibald put the tape in and hit play.

"Sir, this is Luke McDonald. I work as a Secret Service Agent for Lisa. Yes sir. She told me to call you if I needed any help."

Archibald looked at the two agents. "Can you use that and protect me?" Archibald asked. The two agents assured him that he was safe. Archibald smiled.

"Gentlemen, this is great cooperation. If I may; you know I own many financial institutions, and I think I need to forgive the loans of those who serve the public every day. May I make you two my first, of many, whose loans are forgiven because they serve and protect this country?"

The two men looked at each other.

"Ah," Archibald said. "I think you're worried how things could look?" The two agents nodded. "How about we just don't tell anyone." Archibald snapped his fingers and his lawyer came over. "I need you to look into these two gentlemen's private student loans and forgive them," Archibald said. The lawyer nodded and took down some information from the two agents. Archibald took a drag off of his cigar. I may have lost Chet, he thought, but I have two more who are more loyal than he ever was.

John and Jessica
The Moores

Chapter 79

As John and Jessica were helping Rosa out of the car, Chet and Trip pulled up to the Moores. Arthur came outside. He had a concerned look on his face.

"John," Arthur began, "What is going on?"

"This young lady may have the motherload of evidence on Archibald," John answered. Arthur's face nearly split with a smile with that information.

"Well, come inside then, dear," Arthur beamed. "Consider yourself a guest as long as you need to be." John touched Arthur at the elbow. Arthur turned around and saw John motion to stay back. As Trip passed by John also stopped him. When they were alone, John spoke.

"Look, I know what I'm about to suggest is highly irregular." John turned to Arthur. "Arthur, can we hide Rosa here? I think she might be what we need to bust Archibald, and I believe there is a leak in the FBI that leads straight to Archibald." John looked at Trip after that statement. Trip winced as John said it, but didn't disagree.

"How much does she know, John?" Trip asked. John smiled broadly.

"Archibald thought she couldn't speak English and said anything and everything in front of her." Trip stared at John for a second, and then began to chuckle.

That conceited fool said everything in front of her, didn't he?" Trip asked. John looked down to the ground and then back at Trip.

"Trip, she heard something between Archibald and Veronica. Archibald told Veronica that Bruce killed

186

Thelma." Trip's face went blank. John continued. "Trip, you know it's all inadmissible, it's hearsay. Bruce didn't admit it in front of anyone, it was Archibald saying it." Trip nodded. His face was unreadable. "Trip, for all we know, Archibald knew she could understand English and they said the things they did to set up Bruce." Trip looked at John and slowly nodded. John hated this. He knew from the earlier conversations he had with Trip that Trip believed Bruce was capable of the murder. John just didn't see it, but that was the problem. With Bruce, John couldn't see anything.

Arthur had been listening intently to the conversation.

"Trip," Arthur began. "I will be glad to house this young lady as long as it takes. You know and I know if she did hear something and Archibald thought she couldn't understand English and that soulless ghoul gets ahold of her, we'll never see her alive again."

Trip and John both looked at Arthur.

"Soulless ghoul?" John asked. Arthur laughed.

"Sorry, John, but that man is the epitome of evil," Arthur responded.

Rosa and Madeline came out of the house together. They looked like long lost friends the way they were talking and laughing.

"Uh, Arthur," said John. "She may be staying for a very long time." John pointed behind Arthur to the two ladies. Arthur turned and looked. After a few seconds he turned back to John.

"Did you say she used to be a housekeeper?" Arthur asked. John nodded. "I think I just found a new one. What do you want to bet she's about to get a healthy raise?" Arthur was chuckling. John shook his head, and clasped Arthur on the back. Trip decided to head back to DC along with Chet. Chet started to leave, when he stopped and said something to Trip. Trip nodded. Chet walked back to Arthur.

"Thank you, sir," Chet said holding out his hand. Arthur smiled as he shook it. "I promise you there won't be a need for a second time." Arthur smiled broadly. Jessica hugged Arthur.

"Thank you, Arthur," she said still holding his neck.

"You know it was my idea," John said. Jessica let go of Arthur and punched John on the shoulder.

"You didn't dodge," Jessica said.

"You hit like a girl," John responded. Jessica drew back to swing and John instantly moved.

"Chicken," she said as she walked toward the house with Arthur.

"John," Trip said coming up behind John. "Are you sure you're sane, dating her?" John grinned broadly. He turned to Trip.

"I've never claimed to be sane, Trip," John responded. Trip clapped John on the shoulder and headed toward the car. Chet joined him and they took off to DC. In the morning the group would go question the senator and try and figure out what their next move was. John looked around the estate and then toward the house. He realized his current. . . . girlfriend, for a lack of a better word, was getting very chummy with his dead wife's parents. John shook his head. It sounded like something on a daytime talk show. John headed inside.

Chapter 80

John and Rosa headed into Arthur's study. John and Jessica had agreed, for the time being, that she didn't need to question Rosa. Jessica knew she could get a little carried away, and Rosa hadn't done anything wrong, that they knew of. Jessica was standing in the kitchen with Madeline. They were having a glass of tea and pleasantly chatting.

"I think it's time you and I had a serious talk," Madeline said. Jessica was a little worried. Madeline smiled. "Jessica, if Arthur and I are in any way standing in front of you and John having a relationship . . . please tell us. That young man has been through enough, and you have been like the second daughter we never had. Jessica, Sam thought the world of you. I know she would approve of you two. Now I may have said too much, but I don't think so. I think you needed to hear that, but if I was wrong and overstepped my bounds, then I am sorry." Jessica took a last drink of her tea, and sat down the glass. She was looking down at the glass, trying to gather her thoughts. She looked up at Madeline, smiling.

"Well, since we are going to attack the subject head on, and not dance around it, thank you." Jessica looked Madeline straight in the eye. "I know you or Arthur never meant this, but part of me feels like I'm the outsider, and I know the three of us have had a much better relationship the past three years than you, Arthur and John have. I care for John. I want to see where this thing between us goes, but I don't want to make things worse here for John."

Madeline came over and hugged Jessica. Madeline released her and had one arm around Jessica's shoulders. "As far as I'm concerned you're a part of this family," Madeline said. "Now, what can I tell you about that boy? Trust me; he was a handful before the drinking."

"Well," Jessica began. Madeline smiled. "I was thinking about cooking something for him one of these nights. He's always complaining he can't get a good home cooked meal." Madeline put her hand to her mouth to cover the smile. She started to move toward the other side of the kitchen, Jessica continued. "And he goes on, and on, and on, and on about this food that I've never cooked. I can cook all sorts of things, but . . ." She paused looking at Madeline for the word.

"It doesn't taste like mamma's?" Madeline offered. Jessica nodded. Madeline reached for a book and flipped through the pages for a minute. She pulled out a sheet and handed it to Jessica. Jessica scanned it and her mouth dropped open.

"Fried salmon patties, fried potatoes and onions, white beans, cabbage, and corn bread!" Jessica exclaimed. "Madeline, this is his dream meal! Can I copy this?"

You can have it," Madeline replied. "That was Sam's copy. We had to get it from his mother." She shook her head. "He would always eat anything anyone cooked, but you knew it wasn't what he wanted. In fact, according to Sam, he cooked three quarters of their meals. He's a good boy, he just has a little bit of a strange streak in him." Madeline thought about that for a moment. "Well they all do, don't they." She paused and got a huge smile on her face. "Want me to help you make that?"

"Now?" Jessica asked. Madeline nodded and Jessica grinned broadly. "He would love it. Has he ever tried to make it?"

Madeline laughed out loud. Jessica looked at her in surprise.

"Have you ever seen the man cook?" Madeline asked. Jessica shook her head no. "It's amazing. He can make all sorts of things, but when it comes to his favorite

meal, he absolutely ruins it. It's like he's too excited."
Jessica was silent thinking about that statement and
applying it to a bigger picture. Madeline saw the look on
Jessica's face. She walked over to Jessica and squeezed her
shoulders. "He's a good man Jessica. He's a good man,"
she said quietly.

Chapter 81

John had talked to Rosa for what felt like hours. It was relaxed and informal, but it was still tiresome. Arthur had been there the entire time. John was surprised with some of the things Arthur knew, but maybe he shouldn't have been. John was thinking about wrapping things up, when he caught a scent. He sniffed the air.

"Do you smell that?" He asked, interrupting Rosa. Rosa looked at Arthur who shrugged.

John knew that smell. John knew that smell like he knew the back of his hand. He always felt comfortable when he smelled it. It was home. John had a hard time as a kid with his ability. His parents accepted him and loved him unconditionally. When he was having particularly bad days, his mother would always make him his favorite meal; fried salmon patties, fried potatoes and onions, boiled cabbage, white beans, and cornbread. The smell stirred up feelings inside of him of comfort, safety, and love. He opened the door half expecting to see his mother there, instead he saw Jessica, with the biggest grin in the world on her face. He looked at the table and there it was. John didn't know what to say. He just pointed to the table.

"Now listen," Jessica began. "I don't want you thinking I'm you're little maid or cook, or that I'm going to tidy up after you, but I thought you might like a little comfort food."

John grinned at Jessica and sat down. He took a bite and was instantly happy. He looked at Jessica.

"Jessica, I think I umph." Jessica had sprinted the distance between them and put her hand over his mouth before he could finish the sentence. The look on her face was of complete seriousness. John didn't know what he had done, but it was wrong, and he knew it.

"John," she began, with tears in her eyes. "You don't get to say that. Do you understand? You don't get to say I think before whatever the rest of that sentence was going to be. You either do or you don't. Until you do, you don't say it. You can't take it back once you do. You have to know, and until you know, then you don't know. That made no sense." John was breathing carefully through his nose, his mouth full of food. "Don't say it until you mean it." She backed up and took her hand off his face. "I hope you enjoy it. I'm tired and going to bed, good night."

Jessica took off. John finished chewing and looked around the room. Madeline looked at John with sorrow in her eyes. John stood up and walked up to Arthur.

"Arthur," he began. "I need a favor." Arthur nodded. "I think I need to go find a meeting. Will you drive me?"

"Of course John, of course," Arthur said. They headed out of the house. Madeline began to put things in containers to go into the refrigerator.

"I don't understand," Rosa said. Madeline stopped looked at Rosa and smiled.

"Rosa," Madeline replied. "I don't know if those two understand yet."

Chapter 82

Arthur drove for a little while. He thought he knew where a couple of AA meetings were being held, but since he wasn't a member, he really had no idea. John kept staring out the window.

"You have no idea where we're going do you, Arthur?" John asked.

"No, John. No I don't," he replied. John pointed towards a little coffee shop and Arthur pulled in. "You think we can find out in there?"

"I have no idea," John replied. "But I thought maybe I could sit and you could let me talk for a bit since we can't find one." Arthur nodded. They went inside, found a booth away from everyone. Arthur ordered coffee and John had a glass of water. John started at his water for a minute and then spoke, never looking up from the water.

"Do you remember the Gates case?" John asked.

"The case that got you discredited with the FBI four years ago?" Arthur asked. John nodded.

"I never worked the Gates case," John replied still staring at the water. Arthur looked very confused. "Another agent was actually responsible for the goof. But when Gates got killed there was an emergency meeting with just a few people in the FBI. Originally it was just me and Trip that knew I had nothing to do with the case. There was a plant in the mafia. He was an FBI agent, and he told many made men that I had been paid off and taken out Gates. We used the opening to bring down the whole family."

"I'm sorry, John, made men?"

"Sorry, Arthur, made men are those in the mafia who have taken the blood oath and are now a part of La Cosa Nostra, what we know as the mafia," John replied still staring at his glass of water. "They've taken a blood oath to belong to the organization and die for it before they would

194

tell any of its secrets. This FBI man was just an associate, a non-made member, but he knew the Underboss, or second in command, really well. Anyway, my friend, Mark, convinced them I was on the take. You know about what happened with the FBI. Mark told me I needed to look the part, so I started drinking in bars while I was supposed to be suspended. This was about the time that Chet and Jessica were finally let into the loop. When I was finally cleared by the FBI, the mafia thought they had a G-Man under their thumb."

Arthur sat for a minute. "John, did the Mafia kill Sam?"

John shook his head. "I don't think so, Arthur," he replied. "I don't think they would have killed her and not kill me." John was silent for a few seconds. "Mark died during a disagreement at a strip club. A patron, a made-man, shot Mark. I was told I had to make the problems go away with the shooting, and I did, but I hated it." John harrumphed a laugh. "You know they used to call me "The Saint." I told them I was married and I didn't want any of their girls they had dancing. I was so worried about the things I might have to do to get in their good graces. I told Sam all about it, and Arthur, she was not comfortable with the assignment at all. I promised if it came to it, I would quit before I hooked up with one of the girls. The boss was there one day, Anthony Lucciano. He asked me why I didn't help myself to some of my rewards, so to speak. I told him that I meant no offense to him or anyone there, but I had made a personal vow to my wife that I never planned on breaking. I told him, respectfully, if that was a problem that I would go or whatever they wanted me to do. Tony looked at me and said, 'That's what's wrong with today's Young Turks, no respect for honor or rules. John, if any of these guys give you trouble, they've got trouble with me.' I never had a problem after that."

John paused and continued to stare at the water.

"John, do you want a drink, is that what's wrong?" Arthur asked.

John gave a rueful grin. "Arthur, I always want a drink, but I never want to drink again."

Arthur thought about that for a minute. When he spoke it was very softly. "That must be horrible." John nodded.

"If I had never tried to," John began, but Arthur cut him off.

"Stop, John," Arthur said, slapping his hand against the table. "Stop it now. You did what needed to be done. Sam knew it and loved you for it. Besides, you said yourself, it wasn't the Mafia."

John finally looked up at Arthur. "Arthur, I missed so much because of that bust. It didn't make my career, in fact, it ended it for a long time."

"John," Arthur began. "The world needs you. They need someone to stop the evil that's out there. I know that as soon as you took out Lucciano that someone else took his place. Sam said this to me so many times. She would say, 'Dad, if he doesn't stop them, then who will, and would you trust them the way you do John to take them down. How many have we known that have been bought out by corruption?' John, you are the best at what you do, and you can't stop. In fact, I am asking you, please don't stop."

Chapter 83

John sat there for a second, silent. He nodded once and moved the water out from in front of him.

"Arthur, I don't want to do to Jessica what I did to Sam," John said quietly.

"Well, so far you're doing the exact same thing," Arthur said pointing a finger in John's face. John's jaw dropped. "You pushed Sam away at the end so she wouldn't get hurt: what do you think you're doing to Jessica? And don't give me that crap about how you've only been dating for a few weeks. John, you've known that girl for years. Sam told me several times if something ever happened to her she was sure you two would be great together. Boy, what is your problem? You've been alone for three years, she is an amazing woman."

"Do you know how many people have all told me the same thing?" John asked, grinning. "She is amazing, and quite attractive."

"She's also got one devastating right hook," Arthur replied.

"Did she swing at you?" John asked.

"No, but I saw the shot she took at you," Arthur said. "John, I'll listen all night to you if I need to, but can we go home?"

John got up and headed toward the door, with Arthur following him. They went outside and headed toward the car

"Do you think they kept the food?" John asked.

Arthur smiled. "John, there is no way Madeline would have thrown that out," he replied.

"Good," John said. "That was as good as mom's." John paused before he opened the car door. "You're good with me and Jessica, right?"

"Sam wouldn't have it any other way John, and neither would I."

Chapter 84

John and Jessica were heading to see Jeremiah and Bruce in the hospital. The car ride had been silent; awkwardly silent. John decided to break the silence.

"So, the food was really good last night," John said, staring straight ahead.

"Oh," Jessica replied never taking her eyes off of the road. "I thought you left shortly after I went upstairs."

"Arthur took me to find a meeting," John said. Jessica's eyes darted toward John, but she never turned her head. John continued. "We couldn't find one, so we went to a diner and I talked some things out. When we got back, I ate it. It was really good."

"You said that," Jessica replied, not for sure how to deal with the meeting comment.

"You made me realize something last night," John said.

"Oh," Jessica said still staring straight ahead.

"I'm not being fair to you." John turned and looked straight at Jessica. Jessica glanced at him for a second, and silently rebuked herself. "There are going to be times in my life when I'm going to have to go to a meeting. I need you to know it's not necessarily your fault, or that you did something, but I will need to go. I hope you can deal with that." Jessica pursed her lips and nodded.

"So I guess I owe you a meal when we get back to New York," John said trying to change the subject.

"Oh," Jessica replied. "What are you going to make, fried bologna sandwiches and a pickle spear?" she said sarcastically.

John paused for a second. "That sounds good actually," John said.

"It does," Jessica begrudgingly replied.

"What would you know about fried bologna?"

"John," Jessica said looking him in the eye for a split second and then turning back to the road. "Do you have a clue where I'm from?"

"It's not from the South."

"Kentucky is not the South," Jessica stated flatly.

"Don't tell the people of Kentucky that," John said shaking his head. Jessica started to chuckle. "Let me guess, you had family from the South and that's where you had first had fried bologna?"

Jessica smiled and kept driving. After a minute she spoke quietly. "I want a world famous John Cheeseburger Pizza that Sam was always raving about." John was a little taken aback.

"You know I don't use real pizza crust?" He asked.

"I know," she replied with a satisfied smirk on her face. "I listen to my friends."

"And I don't?" John protested.

"Reading someone is not listening to them," Jessica retorted. John licked his finger and drew a point on an imaginary scoreboard. "It's a few more than that," Jessica said grinning broadly at John. John smiled back and settled into the seat, watching the scenery go by.

Luke McDonald
Baltimore, Maryland

Chapter 85

Luke picked up the burner phone and called the cell phone number preprogrammed in it for the tenth time. The phone on the other end rang and rang with no answer. Luke disconnected the call, and knew it was time to take care of himself. He began to work on the explosive device. He needed something for leverage, and this was the only thing that he could think of. Luke had explosive training from his days in the military.

It was obvious that Archibald had turned on him, or was just going to let him hang out to dry. No, Archibald wouldn't do that. Archibald had a backup plan, and Luke was sure it contained a way to make sure he couldn't tell how Archibald was involved. When he finished the bomb, he was going to call John Fowler and turn himself in. Luke had to make sure he came in protected. Luke wasn't sure who Archibald's man was in the FBI, but Luke was certain a kill order had been put out on him.

Luke knew his only chance was to tell everything he knew on Archibald and try to get into witness protection. Luke hadn't actually kidnapped the senator, so that should play into his favor. Luke knew the Attorney General from his years in the White House, and he knew that telling all on Archibald wouldn't keep Luke from not serving any jail time, but it was the only way Luke thought he was going to come out of this situation alive. Luke pushed all the thoughts about Archibald from his mind. He had to finish this explosive in case the mole in the FBI came in to take him out before John could get to Luke's location. Luke swore to himself that he would never chase another woman like Lisa if he ever got out of this mess alive.

Washington DC Hospital
Senator Cosby's Room

Chapter 86

John and Jessica entered the senator's hospital room. Bruce was in the chair beside his father. John couldn't believe the change that had come over Bruce in the past few days. John had never seen Bruce show any compassion for anyone before.

"Learn anything?" John asked Bruce. Bruce shook his head no.

"I haven't asked much," Bruce replied. "I figured I'd wait until Jessica gets here; just as long as she remembers he isn't a suspect." Jessica shot Bruce a withering look, and Bruce smiled back at her. John was in shock. Bruce seemed like a regular guy. Jessica came over and hugged the senator.

"Like I could ever grill this guy," Jessica said, still embracing the senator.

"Now, my dear," the senator began, with tears in his eyes. "You mustn't worry about me; I'm a tough old bird." John smiled at the senator. "You better not hug me too long Jessica." Jessica let go and looked at him. "We wouldn't want to make your boyfriend insanely jealous." John laughed at loud. Jessica shook her head, smiling.

"He's not my boyfriend, Jeremiah," Jessica replied, glancing over her shoulder at John. "He hasn't had the good sense to make that move."

"Is there something wrong with him?" The Senator asked.

"Hey!" John exclaimed, in mock annoyance. "I'm standing right here!" Jessica went on, ignoring him.

"I think he's got commitment issues," Jessica said, straightening the senator's gown.

"Is there someone else?" The senator asked quietly. John threw up his arms in frustration. Jessica gave the senator a withering look.

"He's not that stupid," she said. Jeremiah roared with laughter. Bruce watched the whole exchange, with hate slowly growing in him. Here was another trying to push her way into his father's life. Bruce checked himself discreetly to not give any of his emotions away. First it was his illegitimate . . . no he wouldn't give her that recognition. Bruce had to take care of a few loose ends in this case, and then it might be time to take care of John once and for all . . . and if Jessica should get involved, then he would take care of her too. John spoke, breaking Bruce from his thoughts.

"I hear you're about to get a job promotion," John said trying to change the subject of him and his love life, or lack thereof.

Bruce beamed with pride. "May I have the pleasure of introducing you to the future Vice-President of the United States of America . . . my dad . . . Jeremiah Cosby." Jeremiah smiled and squeezed Bruce's hand. John just couldn't get over how things had changed with Bruce. Bruce smiled proudly and thought of all the different ways he would soon get rid of John.

Chapter 87

"Look," John said. "While I'm extremely happy to see you and hear about your new advancement in the political arena, the clock's ticking on your kidnapper getting away, Jeremiah. Do you have any idea who might have kidnapped you?"

"Party pooper," Jessica said glancing over her shoulder at John and giving him a withering look. John shrugged his shoulders as if to say, "What did I do?"

"Okay, okay you two," Jeremiah said, waving his hand at them to get them to quit. "The only thing I know is one of the kidnappers said something about Luke being behind the kidnapping."

Jessica and John exchanged a look. That sounded like a set-up to both of them. Bruce leaned down beside his dad.

"Are you sure, dad?" he asked.

"Of course I am, Son, you don't forget something like that," Jeremiah replied. Bruce put his hand on Jeremiah's shoulder, trying to comfort him. Jessica patted Jeremiah's hand and smiled at him. She got up and walked toward the door, touching John's shoulder for him to follow her. They stepped outside the room.

"You thinking what I'm thinking?" Jessica asked.

"That I didn't know if was possible for Bruce to have a heart and a soul?" John responded, smiling. Jessica smiled and lightheartedly punched at his shoulder. John didn't dodge and she hit him. Jessica looked at him with an arched eyebrow. John shrugged.

"Different circumstances now," John said simply. Jessica stepped back and stared at John.

"You're saying I was flirting with you by hitting you back then?" She asked. She started to wag her finger. "Un-uh. That was me being friendly, that's all. You know, the way two guys might hit each other when their goofing around. It was just my way of saying we're friends."

"First off," John said, closing his fingers around her still wagging fingers. "You only do that wagging thing when you block a shot in basketball," Jessica smiled in spite of herself. "Secondly," John continued. "Did you ever hit Chet, or Trip, or Bruce, or any other man that way?"

"No," Jessica said. "But I don't have the relationship . . . ." She stopped her sentence before John made something out of it that she didn't mean, but she was already too late.

"No?" John asked, smiling. "I'm begging you, please finish that thought."

"I hate you," Jessica said, her eyes narrowing.

"I can live with that," John said, moving in to kiss her, and he did. John thought he saw fireworks go off, or maybe that was just in his head. He was really afraid he was starting to fall in love. The thought terrified him, and excited him; all at the same time. When John broke the kiss he spoke quietly.

"You didn't try to dodge that," he said grinning. Jessica grinned back.

"I didn't want to," she replied. "Are you going to dodge this?" And with that, she leaned in to kiss him, but stopped when she heard a, "harrumph!"

Jessica spun around and John straightened up. Trip and Chet were standing there. Chet was trying to appear interested in the ceiling tiles. Trip simply shook his head.

"Do we have anything?" Trip asked.

"I don't know, you interrupted us before I could find out," John replied, and then doubled over from the elbow he caught in the ribs from Jessica. Trip held his composure, but his eyes began to water from holding back the laughter.

"One of the men who held Jeremiah said that Luke was his boss," Jessica replied. "I don't know Trip; it all sounds like a setup to me."

"Tell me about it," John replied, trying to catch his breath. Trip's mouth twitched trying to hold back the laughter.

"There's more where that came from," Jessica said to him under her breath.

"The kiss or the elbow?" John asked at full volume. With that comment, Trip lost it. Jessica tried to appear irritated, but gave up. John gave everyone a second.

"Do you have something for us, Trip?" John asked. Trip nodded, as he tried to compose himself. He took a moment and then spoke.

"I just had a phone call from Archibald Staples, turning over evidence to us!"

Chapter 88

Bruce stepped out the door of his father's room just as Trip finished his sentence.

"What's the evidence, Trip?" Bruce asked. Trip looked down at the floor and then over at John. Bruce grew impatient. "Oh, come on! I have been on this case since the beginning. I admit I made a few mistakes, but I want my father's kidnapper brought to justice."

"What's the difference in him and me, Trip?" John asked. Jessica and Trip both looked sharply at John. "I want to look into Sam's killing, and the whole world has signed off on that, so what's the difference for Bruce to go after whoever kidnapped his dad?"

Jessica looked at Trip, hoping he would come up with anything to keep Bruce and John from going out together again. She didn't trust Bruce, regardless of what John thought. Trip frowned at John, and reluctantly nodded.

"You're right, John. Bruce deserves the chance," Trip said, hating himself for going along with John. Trip turned toward Bruce. "Archibald has received numerous calls from a burned cell phone that we have tracked to a warehouse in Baltimore." John was a little surprised by that news. Trip looked at John and shook his head no. "It's not the same warehouse, it's a little ways away, but very close to the warehouse that Jeremiah was found in. It is one owned by Archibald, and he has given us permission to search it."

Bruce turned to John.

"Are you with me?" Bruce asked. John grinned.

"Let's go check it out and see if we can't wrap this thing up," John replied. They started to go, when Jessica grabbed John's arm.

"Bruce, can you give me five minutes with John?" Jessica asked. "There are some things I need to discuss with him. I'll coordinate with the local LEOs if you need any backup."

Bruce nodded and headed to the parking garage. Trip and Chet went into the senator's room leaving John and Jessica alone.

"What do we need to talk . . . " John began, but was interrupted by Jessica kissing him.

Chapter 89

As much as John was enjoying himself, he knew he had to go. He pulled away from Jessica, but she wouldn't let go of him.

"John," Jessica began. "Do not go with him."

John looked confused.

"Jess," he started to reply, but Jessica interrupted him.

"John, do not go with him," she insisted. "I think he killed Thelma . . ." She paused, not sure how much farther to go. She looked him in the eyes. "You know what you keep telling Trip, Chet, and I that we need to wait to tell you? I think it's time you know," she began.

"You think Bruce killed Sam," John said quietly. Jessica looked up at John, and smiled in spite of herself. John shook his head. "That was good old fashioned police work of listening to all the things you three were saying and weren't saying. That had nothing to do with me reading anyone. Jessica, I don't think he did it, but I'm never going to be able to convince the three of you until we investigate him. That's what we're going to do. Let's say he is the murderer, he's not dumb enough to kill me at that warehouse."

"What if he does though?" She asked frantically. "What if he does and I lose you . . . again?" Jessica said again softly, almost a whisper. John was taken aback by the question, and what was implied.

"Jess . . . Jess, what are you saying?" John asked.

Jessica gave him a withering look.

"Oh no, John," she said, growing angrier by the second. "You don't get to have your ego inflated by thinking I was waiting around for you. You don't get to think that I pined over you like some brainless floozy. You don't get to hold anything like that over me, do you understand me? Do you?" Tears were running down Jessica's face. John was speechless. He went to hold her but she pushed him away. She turned away. She was crying and had her arms crossed in front of her. She composed herself and spoke softly, still looking the other way.

"You know what the worst part is? I would never ever, EVER have asked you to break your vow to Sam. For one thing, I knew you wouldn't hurt her, but for another, you wouldn't, you were committed to her. That's what is so crazy. It's one of the reasons I fell for you so hard. It's who you are, John. You tackle anything and everything that's wrong. You made a commitment to her, and you believed in until death do you part. You took that seriously, and heaven help me, I love you for it."

John didn't say a word, but the question running through his mind was simple, did she love him? For all the reads he could get on people, he just couldn't understand them when they had to do with him and his love life. John decided he had to say something. He said the only thing he knew to say.

"I had no idea, Jess," he said softly.

Jessica laughed. "Typical," she said. "Sam did."

Chapter 90

John played back the sentence Jessica just said several times to make sure he heard what he thought he heard. Jessica turned around and looked at him. She knew he was trying to process what he had just heard. She smiled ruefully.

"She knew, John," Jessica said simply walking towards him. He took his hands in hers.

"I never will forget what she said when I finally told her. She told me she had known for a long time. She also said that we don't choose who we love. She also knew I'd never act on it in a hundred years." She put down his hands and looked down at the ground. When she looked back up, she looked right into his eyes.

"Why do you think I covered you as much as I could the past three years when you had your little outbursts?" She asked. John didn't say anything. "Do you know how many times I almost called you, or knocked on your door? Do you know how many nights I spent watching you watching some of the people you did? And by the way, that private eye job . . ." Jessica just shook her head and shuddered. John grinned at her. "How long do you wait to ask someone out on a date after he told you he hated you? How long do you wait to tell someone who nearly drank himself to death after his wife died . . . how long do you wait to tell him how you feel about him? John, these aren't rhetorical questions."

"I don't know," John said quietly. "I can't figure out why two of the greatest women I have ever met in my life both think I'm something special."

Jessica rolled her eyes. "Oh, come on, John. You ooze charm, you fight for justice, you have so much character at times its sickening, and as much as it pains me to admit, you're not bad looking."

John grinned and rocked back on his heels. "Anything else?" John asked. He quickly dodged, as Jessica swung at his head.

"You could have knocked me out!" John exclaimed.

"I thought you said it was different circumstances just a few minutes ago?" Jessica asked, smirking.

"They just changed again," John replied. John reached out to take Jessica's hands. She didn't stop him. John looked her in the eye.

"You're not going to lose me," he said. Jessica's jaw was trembling. John leaned in close. "You've made the mistake of telling me how much you need me, so I'm going to follow you around like a bad penny. You're stuck with me, Jessica, until you decide to run me off." Jessica grinned.

"Me and my big mouth," she said quietly. John leaned in like he was going to kiss her, and stopped an inch away.

"I don't know what it is I do that makes you feel the way you do about me, but I'm glad you do," John said above a whisper.

"Did I mention charming?" Jessica asked, before she kissed him. Trip and Chet walked out of the senator's room right at that time.

"I mean do you two have nothing else to do?" Trip asked.

"And what if I said we didn't?" John asked letting go of Jessica and walking up to Trip. Trip smiled and clapped John on the back.

"Then I'd say, it's about time," Trip responded. John smiled and turned back to Jessica.

"I need to go search that warehouse," John said. "I will see you later."

"You better," Jessica yelled as John headed down the hall. "If something happens to you I'll haunt you."

John turned and continued walking down the hall backwards. He called back to her, "Don't you have that backwards?"

"Fowler, I meant exactly what I said," she called back.

John smiled, opened the door to the stairwell, and paused. "I believe you," and with that he was gone. Jessica had a sinking feeling that something awful was about to happen.

Chapter 91

John and Bruce arrived at the warehouse address Chet had sent them. They approached the door cautiously. Bruce took the lead, and they cleared each room quietly and efficiently. As they headed deeper into the warehouse, they both thought they heard something.

"FBI!" John yelled. He listened for a response and didn't hear one. They proceeded cautiously. They came into the main spacious room. John heard someone moving something. "FBI!" He yelled again.

"Don't come any closer," came the response.

"Luke, Luke McDonald?" John yelled.

"Yeah, John, is that you?" Luke yelled back.

"Yes it is Luke, now come out with your hands up!" John yelled.

"Are you by yourself?" Luke asked.

Bruce got John's attention. He nodded yes. John wasn't sure what was going on.

"John, listen to me, some people want me dead," Luke said. "I'll turn myself in to you and to you only."

"That's fine with me Luke, I'm here to bring you in. Tell me what happened and we'll see what we can do," John replied.

"John, you don't get it, they want me dead, they'll kill me if they find out I talked," Luke replied.

John walked out where he could see Luke. Luke had his hands up, John relaxed. It was at that time Bruce bumped a container and it made a loud noise. John turned toward the noise. Luke bent down and threw something in John's direction. John turned back to see what he thought was a grenade. John dove away. As the grenade exploded he thought about how mad Jessica was going to be at him.

Chapter 92

John kept hearing a ringing noise. He was also wondering why his face was wet. He put a hand to his nose, and pulled it back. Blood covered his hand. He felt his forehead and it was sticky and wet. John felt his stomach roll. This isn't good, John thought. I think I have a concussion. John felt someone grab his leg and begin to pull him across the floor. His head bumped the concrete when he tried to look up to see what was going on.

"Ow!" John exclaimed. Bruce tried to help John up, but John was seeing two of him. John's stomach rolled again and he thought he would throw up.

"You okay?" Bruce asked. John couldn't quite make out what Bruce was saying due to the ringing in his ears. He was quite sure Bruce had either asked him if he wore a toupee or if he wanted hay, but John had no idea why Bruce would be asking questions like that at a time like this.

"The next one won't miss!" Luke yelled.

John tapped Bruce on the shoulder. Bruce turned around and yelled "GRENADE!" in John's ear. That he heard.

"I've got a bomb!" Luke yelled. "Have John come and arrest me, or I set it off!"

John still couldn't make out what was being said, but he knew he had heard the word bomb. Bruce was looking at something and sighting it with his gun. John had a bad feeling about what Bruce was about to do.

"John," Bruce said turning back to him. "I can take out the bomb. He's going to set it off. He's gone crazy. We need to stop him. I can shoot it without us getting hurt."

"Bruce," John said, wiggling his finger in his ear. "I'm not hearing too well right now, but I swore you just said you were going to shoot a bomb."

216

Bruce nodded. John grabbed Bruce by his shoulders.

"Are you nuts? That thing could go off and kill us all!" John screamed.

"Let John come arrest me and I'll tell everything!" Luke yelled.

"What did he say?" John asked. "I can't hear right."

"He's going to set it off if we come any closer. John you're hurt and I'm not letting him get away." Bruce was pleading with John. John was having trouble hearing anything Bruce was saying, and he was really having trouble reading lips. John felt his stomach roll and bent over, thinking he was going to hurl. Bruce saw this as an opportunity and stood, aiming. Luke saw who was with John, and his heart sank.

"Bruce," Luke whispered to himself. He then began to shout. "Bruce! Don't! I won't tell them anything!"

"You're right, you won't," Bruce said quietly to himself. Bruce fired as Luke started to run. John realized what was about to happen and tried to take cover. As the bomb exploded all John could think was he was about to see Sam a whole lot faster than he had planned . . . that and Jessica was going to kill him for getting himself killed.

Chapter 93

It was dark. John was sure he was dead. He didn't hear the ringing in his head anymore. That was good.

"Sam?" He asked, hoping for once in his life she wouldn't answer. He waited a minute and when there was no answer, he decided to chance it

John opened his eyes and looked up. He saw the sky. This was the second time in just a few minutes he found himself flat on his back and not quite sure how he had gotten there. He heard sirens all around him. Something was wrong, but he couldn't quite figure out what. It dawned on him he was in a warehouse, but now he could see the sky. He could feel the concrete underneath him, but he was presently concerned about what had happened to the roof of the warehouse. John tried to lift his head to see, but decided it hurt way too much. He shut his eyes for a second and listened to the sirens approach. He heard footsteps approach him. John groaned.

"Lying on your back while you let your partner make the big collar, John?" Jessica asked.

"Is there anything left of Luke to collar?" John asked. Jessica paused before she answered. John opened his eyes and looked up at her. He thought he might have a concussion; that or she was an angel with the weird glow around her. Jessica slowly shook her head. "Bruce?" John asked.

"Oh, he's outside. Apparently he went to help you, according to him, but you told him to let you lay here and die. Bruce wasn't sure if you were injured and should be moved so he called for an ambulance." Jessica got down on one knee and whispered. "There isn't enough evidence to go after Bruce for Luke's death, or anyone else's. Trip wants to keep an eye on him."

John nodded. "I think he actually might have saved my life and his by shooting that bomb. Jessica, I don't think he's the killer." He paused a second. "You're mad at me aren't you?" Jessica just stared at him. "I'm going to have to pay for this aren't I?"

Jessica nodded and smiled at him. John smiled back and started to lean up to kiss her. John stopped from the pain, and began to groan. Jessica punched him on the arm.

"Oh knock it off, you big baby," she said.

"Jessica! I could be concussed!" John exclaimed.

"Do you want to spend the night in the hospital, or ride with me back to your in-laws and we stay there and rest up for a day or so?" Jessica asked. John sat straight up.

"Faker," Jessica said, smiling.

"I'm really hurting," John replied, trying to look pitiful. Jessica put an arm around John's shoulders and whispered in his ear.

"Do you need a sponge bath?" John looked her in the eyes and nodded. She pushed his head to where she could whisper into his ear again. "Do you need me to kiss your owies and make them better?" John looked into her eyes again, and nodded. Jessica backed up. She began to speak very slowly and sensually. "You know," she paused, and looked at him mischievously. She continued. "I know this male nurse . . ."

"You're mean," John said getting to his feet. He started to walk out of the building. He looked up and noticed that part of the roof had been blown off. That would explain the big hole he saw from his back earlier, he thought. They walked outside and saw Bruce. He was talking with Trip. Trip saw them and waved them off.

"Go to the Moores, take a couple days off. We'll take care of paperwork when you get back," Trip yelled. John nodded and locked eyes with Trip. Trip nodded at John. John knew Trip wanted to arrest Bruce right here, but there was no evidence of Bruce for any of the murders, and honestly John wasn't sure Bruce was guilty. John started to get into the car when EMTs intercepted him and began to check his various cuts, bruises and overall wellbeing.

As John let the EMTs work on him, his mind wandered. The conversation John and Trip had a few days ago kept running through John's mind. The only people John couldn't get a read on were sociopaths . . . and Bruce. John looked at Bruce, who smiled broadly at John. John nodded and got into the car with Jessica, brooding. Could Bruce be the one responsible for Thelma's death . . . and Sam's?

Chapter 94

John said very little on the trip back to the Moores. There were two reasons for John to return to the Moores. One was to get some rest, and the second was to check back in on Rosa. John was contemplating letting Jessica have a go at Rosa, but Rosa didn't deserve to be treated like a suspect. John was afraid if he didn't let Jessica do what she did best that Archibald would slip away. He wasn't sure what to do.

While John was contemplating all of this, Jessica had been watching John and thinking about how much he was complicating her life. She had to admit she didn't like John going with Bruce to go after Luke, but she wouldn't have liked that even if they weren't . . . well, whatever they were. Jessica glanced at John again and decided she had had enough!

"John," she began. "We need to talk."

"Okay," he replied.

"The last case we were on, I nearly told off the director because of how you made me feel. Tonight I was scared to death about you being with Bruce," she held up her hand to cut him off before he could retort. "I know you think Bruce isn't what Trip, Chet, and I think he is, but when I saw you lying there . . ." She stopped talking for a second trying to gather her thoughts. When she continued she spoke very softly. "I've never felt like this before."

John grinned. "You've got it pretty bad, huh?" he asked quietly. Jessica rolled her eyes. John continued. "That took some guts sharing that."

Jessica wasn't expecting that response. She was prepared to fire off a retort, but she was taken by surprise.

"So what do you want me to do?" John asked.

"I want you to tell me how you feel," Jessica replied quietly.

"I feel like you've kept me out of harm's way for three years. I feel like you were my partner, the better looking of the two of course, and I feel like I can trust you with my life. I feel like you might be the only person on Earth that I can trust with my heart." John paused. "I think I'm falling for you, and I don't know how to be what you deserve, and I think you deserve better than me. I think I'm going to have to work very hard to ever be close to what you deserve, and I think I want to do that." John was very silent, and then asked very quietly, "What do you think?"

"I think I want to pull this car off of the road and make out with you," she replied. John gulped, audibly. Jessica laughed and then continued. "However, due to your current injuries, I think I want to take it safe. I mean I wouldn't want to overexcite your system or anything."

"I'm willing to take the risk," John replied. Jessica smiled at John. John felt his heart pounding in his chest. He had loved Sam. He still did, but he wasn't for sure anyone had ever made him feel like this.

"Calm down, John," Jessica said playfully.

"What?"

"You look like you might stroke out over there. Look let's go to the Moores, you get a day or two of rest, and then we figure this out, together."

"Oh, crap," John said.

"What's wrong?"

"I promised Arthur I'd tell him everything when this was all over," John replied, looking very uncomfortable.

Jessica nodded. She reached over and took John's hand.

"I know," she said smiling. "Madeline told me all about the deal you made with Arthur. You and I are going back to New York in a couple of days, get all the files on Sam. I've already talked to Trip and Chet. They have agreed to join us here, and we'll tell them everything we know." Jessica paused. "John; Trip, Chet, and I have to tell you things about Sam you don't know. We have to tell you all the things we've been keeping from you since we pulled you out of your private eye life." John smiled and nodded. He knew this had been coming. Jessica continued. "After all that, if you'll let us, the three of us would like to help you solve your wife's murder."

John smiled at Jessica and nodded. He was looking forward to a day off. It had been a trying couple of weeks. In two weeks he had done more than most agents did at the peak of their career. John had been basically retired three weeks ago, and now he was closing big cases again. It was a major change to his life. He really needed to go to an AA meeting when he got back to New York; in fact, he might try and find one tomorrow night here in Virginia. John leaned back in his seat and watched the sights go by. In less than a week they were going to reopen his wife's case. Maybe I should find a meeting tonight, John thought.

That Night
Psychiatric Hospital

Chapter 95

Pamela was working the night shift the way she always did; studying. She hoped she passed her test the next morning. This was the last pre-requisite class for her to get into the doctorate of nursing program. She had always wanted to be a nurse practitioner. She hated her job here. She wanted to help people, but the people here . . . they had problems, problems that Pamela wasn't ready to cope with. Honestly, she was scared many nights at her job, especially since the new patient had been added to her floor, David George.

All he did the past few nights was sing some song about Lisa. He seemed so normal during the day, but at night . . . at night he terrified her. She was positive he wasn't taking his meds, but she couldn't prove it, and none of the doctors paid any attention to her. She was simply in charge of watching the security monitors at night and putting the facility on lockdown if she saw someone trying to escape. She hadn't been disturbed but a few times in all of the years working here. Tonight was going to be one of those nights she was disturbed. A man came up to her and flashed an FBI badge.

"I'm Special Agent John Fowler with the FBI," the man said. "I have to talk to David George right this second. It is imperative to national security!"

"I'll have to call my supervisor," Pamela answered.

"Perhaps you didn't hear me," the man said, angrily. "That man was charged in the attempted kidnapping of the first lady. We have to know exactly how he entered into the White House. Other countries may try to duplicate his attempt. We have to seal this leak immediately!" The agent leaned in close. "This is for the safety of our country."

Pamela jumped up and headed down the hall with her keys. David was in a locked room for his protection and for the protection of those around him. Pamela unlocked the door, and turned toward the agent.

"Anything else?" she asked.

"I'm going to have to take him with me," the agent said, handing her some papers. "I don't have all the paperwork right now, but the FBI should be sending it down in the next few days. If you don't receive what you need by the end of the week, you need to contact the FBI and ask for John Fowler."

Pamela looked at the paperwork, and saw all that was missing was the judge's signature. She looked back up at the agent.

"Our judge is on vacation, he won't be back for two days. Just start the paperwork process and everything you need will be here by the end of the week." Pamela nodded. The agent put handcuffs on David George, who was smiling broadly.

"Good to see you again, Agent FOWLER," David stressed, still smiling. The agent pulled David along and they went out of the building. David was put in the back of the car. The agent opened his door, and waved at Pamela. Pamela smiled; glad to see David George gone.

Chapter 96

The car drove down the road with David George in the back. He was humming a tuneless song. After a few minutes, the car pulled over to the side of the road.

"Is this where you kill me?" David George asked.

"Now why would I do that?" Bruce asked.

"Well," David began. "I have no idea who you are or why you would break me out. I figured Archibald sent you to have me taken out."

"That's an interesting theory," Bruce replied. "Have you ever heard the old saying, the enemy of my enemy is my friend?" David nodded. "Then consider us friends."

Bruce picked up a bag from the front seat and pitched it into the back.

"In there is money, a few survival items, and a key to locker, with an address on it. At that address are a few other weapons to help you in your crusade against the Staples. You see, David, they tried to screw me over, and then they had the audacity to send someone else in to help me." Bruce looked very offended as he spoke. "Like I need any help from anyone! I have a few loose ends to take care of, and then I am going to disappear, with or without my Daddy's blessing. This is your chance to take care of the thorn in your side."

David sat there for a minute, slowly nodding.

"So any chance you have a change of clothes for me?" Bruce smiled, and got out of the car. He opened David's door, and helped him out. Bruce took the handcuffs off of David and opened the trunk. In the trunk was a change of clothes. The road was deserted, so David changed right there. David laced up his boots, grabbed the bag Bruce had given him and looked around.

"There's a small town about 3 miles that way," Bruce said, pointing.

"Which way is the address of the weapons locker?" David asked. Bruce pointed in the opposite direction. "Then that's the way I'll go," David said. He started walking and stopped. "You know he's going to find out."

Bruce smiled at David. "I'm counting on it.

David shook his head at Bruce. "Do you think you can take him out?" David asked. Bruce smiled a million watt smile.

"He's been a dead man walking for weeks and didn't even know it," Bruce replied.

"While I owe you for helping me out, I have to tell you, you don't stand a chance against Fowler. Good luck," and with that, David was off. He slipped into the fog and night. Bruce stood there for a minute scowling. He got back in the car, thinking about David George. Bruce had to take down John, but not yet . . . not yet.

Two Days Later
NY FBI Building

Chapter 97

Dr. Freeman was in his office when he received the text that changed his life. The text simply contained two words, All clear. Stephen wasn't sure how to act. For the past twenty years he had been under Duck's thumb. There was a time in Stephen's life when he loved to bet on the ponies. Stephen knew he had devised a system in which he could never lose; until he did. He kept trying to win money to pay back his bookie, but it never worked. He started sports betting and for a while Stephen was catching up, until the "earthquake series" in the 90s. Stephen knew he could never pay off what he owed, and so did Robert Mariotti, the man known as the Duck.

Today he was known as the alleged head of organized crime, but before that he was a loan shark. Duck was a genius who knew how to collect on the vig, or interest on a loan. Duck used his clients to get information that he could turn into a profit. Sometimes he loaned one of his clients out in return for a payment. Duck would put a percentage of that payment toward the principal of the loan, creating a win-win for all parties; at least that was how it was originally described to Stephen.

Stephen thought he had gotten out of debt to Duck a few years ago when he finally found a bank that was willing to give Stephen a loan to pay back the loan shark. What Stephen didn't know at the time, and soon found out, was the president of the bank was in Duck's pocket. Stephen had almost given up hope of ever getting out from under all the money he owed.

Over the years Stephen noticed that he was doing things that in the beginning of their arrangement he would have never agreed to. This had been Stephen's last job, and he was grateful. He was sure that his actions in Trip's office a few nights ago had led to the death of Trip's girlfriend.

Stephen picked up his hat and gathered his papers. Tomorrow the orders would come down that Stephen was to be transferred. Stephen didn't know who Duck owned in the hierarchy of the FBI, but he was absolutely sure that there was someone. Stephen was scared John was on to him, and the sooner he got out of New York, the better. He went to the door, opened and took one last look around the office. Stephen shook his head; he would be back tomorrow to clean up, it wasn't like this was the last time he would see this office. Stephen closed the door to his New York office for the last time.

Chapter 98

Dr. Freeman started across the parking garage floor. As he was walking, he noticed there was a van parked near the security camera. He found it odd that the workmen left the camera without having it fixed. Stephen shrugged. With budgets being constantly scrutinized and gone through with fine tooth combs, he really wasn't surprised, but he did find it odd. As he got to his car, he got the feeling that someone was watching him. Stephen looked around, but didn't see anyone. There were very few cars left in the parking lot. Stephen chuckled, with only a handful of cars in the lot; one would be parked right next to his. Stephen paused before he opened the door to his car. He had a nagging suspicion that someone was under the vehicle parked next to his. He got in the car quickly, locked the doors, and looked down toward the car beside him. He saw no movement. Stephen chuckled and leaned back in his seat. He blew out a sigh. That's when the gloved hand covered his mouth and nose.

Stephen was struggling. His air was being cut off by the hand and now an arm snaked across his neck. He felt hot breath against his neck. Stephen was seeing black spots. His mind spun. Then he heard a voice.

"Steve, ole buddy, I really hate to have to do this . . . but I have to send a message to your boss. No one! And I mean NO ONE crosses me!"

Stephen tried to answer, to no avail. Suddenly Stephen felt sweet air rush into his lungs. Then Stephen felt nothing as his neck cracked.

"When are people going to learn?" Bruce asked to the dead body in the front seat of the car. "When are they going to learn?"

Chapter 99

Bruce hummed to himself. He got out of the car, walked over to the van and opened the door. The smell of gasoline reeked out of the van; it was saturated inside. Bruce pulled out a gas can and began to methodically soak the inside of the car. He was 95% sure no one would be down in the garage, but he wanted to hurry all the same, just in case.

After he was satisfied that the car had been properly soaked, he placed the small explosive inside the car. It was amazing what kind of instructions you could find online these days. He was glad he had destroyed that computer he used with a sledge hammer and then had it crushed at a junk yard. You just can't be too careful these days. He peeled off the coveralls, coverings for his shoes, and his gloves. He threw them all in Stephen's car. He knew he smelled like gas, but that could quickly be corrected. He walked over to a stairwell and headed down to street level quickly. He exited the building out a side door no one used and joined the crowd heading to his gym. He had practiced the route several times over the past week, and was never spotted on any of the security cameras.

As he approached the door to his gym, he slid his hand into his pants pocket and pushed the send button, and listened. He smiled as he heard the faint explosion and went inside. He quickly hurried to his locker. He grabbed his shower gear and washed himself thoroughly. He knew he smelled of gas, but he had made a big scene earlier in the day when he was filling his car of spilling gas. He knew the two attendants on service would remember him if they were ever questioned.

Bruce finished his shower and dressed quickly. Bruce was running things through his mind as he headed to the lot where his secondary car was hidden. The van had been stolen and had been in an impound lot. Bruce had switched plates on the van and parked it in the FBI building with everything he needed a few days ago when the cameras first went down due to "technical difficulties". He moved the van just a few minutes before Stephen had come downstairs to his car. Bruce had swiped Stephen's car keys a few days earlier and made a copy.

Bruce shook his head. He knew his FBI career was over, unless he finished off John. John was determined to find Sam's killer, and that just wouldn't do. Bruce chuckled to himself. The best part of the whole thing was Stephen helped Bruce with his escape. Bruce had gone to Stephen asking to be approved for time off due to his father's kidnapping and emotions that Bruce needed to "deal with." Of course Stephen signed off. He thought they both were working for Archibald. Bruce laughed out loud. Bruce only worked for himself. The fact the "shrink" had never figured that one out was a mistake that had cost Stephen his life.

Bruce realized he was by the river. He parked his car, got out, dropped the small detonator to the ground and crushed it. He then scooped up all the parts and began to throw them into the river. Bruce knew where to go. He had left enough clues for John to figure it out. The next time they met face to face it would be the two of them in a death match.

Bruce reached into his coat pocket and pulled out a small cloth bag closed by drawstrings. He opened the bag and pulled out the simple gold ring with the inscription, "Always yours, John," engraved inside of it. Bruce began to talk to the ring.

"We already know that I'm 1-0 when it comes to Fowlers, don't we Sam?" Bruce asked the ring. He studied the ring for a minute and then spoke his ritual softly.

"If I had a sister, I wouldn't miss her," Bruce said. He put the ring in the bag, and the bag back in his coat. "I'm going to kill you, John, just like I killed that pretty wife of yours. I'm going to frame you for her death, and

I'm going to become the FBI super-agent." Bruce's voice was getting louder and louder. "And then, John, and then. . . and then I'm going to tell my father everything I did for him, and if he doesn't appreciate it. . . well, I'm going to kill him too!" Bruce laughed loudly for several minutes. When he finished he got in his car and prepared to drive as he began to go through his master plan in his head.

Chapter 100

John still couldn't believe what had happened. He and Jessica had been in her office, talking. Well, talking was't really what most would call it. They were shamelessly flirting. Ever since their discussion in the car a few days ago, John thought that their relationship had begun to pick up steam. John knew he had to stop doing that at work, but it was hard. At work; there was a phrase John hadn't said without disdain in a very, very long time.

John snapped back to the present. He was downstairs in the parking garage. Trip had joined them. He hadn't left the building yet; Trip hardly left the building until very late in the evening. Trip saw John and Jessica and waved them over.

"It's Stephen's car, and we're pretty sure Stephen is inside," said Trip.

Jessica went to take a look at the car. She came back, faced Trip and nodded. John was watching Trip and Jessica very closely. They both turned towards John. John raised his eyebrows questioningly.

"Is there something I should know?" John asked.

Trip sighed. He started to say something and his phone rang. He looked at the phone and walked off, taking the call. By the sound of his tone and his body posture, John was pretty sure Trip was talking to someone at the top. What surprised John was that Trip seemed to be telling whoever was on the other end of the line what was going to happen and not the other way around.

"You really just can't resist, can you, John?" Jessica asked.

John turned back toward Jessica, with a smirk on his face. He shrugged his shoulders.

"It just takes over sometimes," John replied. "What is going on here?"

Jessica looked over at the shell of the car. She looked back over towards Trip. Trip was coming back toward them. Jessica waited on Trip.

"We think Stephen might have been a mole," Jessica said. John waited. Jessica leaned towards John nodding her head, thinking John didn't understand. John nodded his head up and down slowly.

"Okay," John said. "What's the big secret?"

"What?" Jessica asked, as quietly as she could so it wouldn't be heard but by the three of them. "How? How could you possibly know?"

John sighed. This was the frustrating part of his ability. To John things seemed so black and white. He just knew things, and it was hard to remember that others didn't see the same things he did. It suddenly dawned on Trip how John knew. Trip almost visibly smacked his forehead.

"You found the whole thing fishy when you were made to go to see Stephen?" Trip asked. John nodded. "But how could you have known by just that?"

"Trip, I'm an old-school investigator. That's what everyone seems to forget," John said. "Just because I figure something out by body language or whatever it is, at the end of the day, it's just a direction I know to look in. I do try to find actual evidence to back things up." John looked over at the burned wreck of the vehicle. "When I saw him it felt like he was trying to make me think Chet was a mole. Then there were little things that he did that set off my internal . . ." John paused looking for the word, "alarm. But the final straw was when I mentioned 'The Duck'. Stephen never asked how he got the name. All of those things made me think it was worth looking into Stephen's financials. Arthur cut through the red tape quickly and found out Stephen was more than maxed out in loans. I was positive Stephen was Archibald's mole. I left it alone, because I wanted to feed misinformation to Archibald. Apparently he did something wrong in Archibald's eyes."

Jessica put her hand over her mouth to stifle a laugh. John turned toward her questioningly.

"For once," Jessica began. "I think your wrong on who had Stephen killed."

Chapter 101

"There are some similarities here to two other murder cases John," Jessica said. John's face got serious real quick. Jessica didn't say anything. John pressed his lips together and shook his head no. Jessica tilted her head slightly, and nodded yes.

"I don't know in what secret language you two are speaking, but here's what I know," Trip began. "Bruce was in the area when all three suspects were killed. We cannot locate Bruce's original file. The one currently on file has been doctored. Bruce got Stephen today to sign off on a leave of absence to deal with his father's kidnapping." That bit of information caused John to look at Trip sharply.

"What are you two trying to say?" John asked quietly, staring at the floor. "Are you saying I've been working with a guy for a week that killed my wife, and because I didn't get a feeling on him that I let him get away? Are you saying that I may have let him walk, and I'm never going to catch the guy? Because if what you have told me is true . . . then that is what I'm saying. I'm saying this is my fault."

"I am saying," Trip said very quietly. "We are keeping this murder under wraps. I am saying I have a person of interest in all three murder cases that are currently being run by Agent Hammerstein. I am saying that all four of us are going to your in-laws house, and we have a chance to interview some people who might have some knowledge of the killer that they don't realize they have." Trip reached out and put his hand on John's shoulder. John looked up at Trip, directly in the eye. "I am saying John, Bruce is a person of interest in the murder of your wife, my girlfriend, and the late Dr. Freeman."

Jessica took Johns free arm into hers. She placed her chin on his shoulder for a second, and then lifted it off. She spoke softly.

"If it's Bruce," she said. "We are going to nail him, I promise." She looked at Trip. "Same goes for you Trip, I promise we'll nail him."

Trip smiled ruefully, "I know you will, Agent Hammerstein, I know you will." Trip looked back over to the car. "You two go. I'll meet you at the Moore's. I'll bring the latest file on this, Jessica." Trip turned and went back to the crime scene.

"You ready?" Jessica asked.

"I need to do something in the morning, Jessica. I need to go to Sam's gravesite for a minute. There's something I need to say to her," John said without ever looking at her. John stared at the car. He was thinking. Could it really be Bruce? If it was, did he miss it because Bruce really was a sociopath, or was it because John didn't want to have to face Sam's killer?

Chapter 102

Chet watched Jessica and John leave. He really didn't think this was the time for John to find out about Stephen. Chet walked over to Trip and tapped him lightly on the shoulder. Trip turned around. Chet gestured with his head to follow him. The two of them walked away from the crime scene, and Chet handed Trip the folder.

"What did you find?" Trip asked as he began to leaf through it.

"You were right, Stephen was in debt. Worse than I ever thought about being," Chet replied. Trip looked up at Chet. Trip was frowning.

"You're lucky, you know," Trip said. Chet nodded.

"I know. That could have been me if I had continued down the road I was heading," Chet replied. He stuck his hands in his pockets and looked down at the ground. Trip looked back over at the crime scene.

"We've got to sit on this," Trip said. Chet's jaw dropped. Trip didn't look happy, but continued. "We can't let Archibald or Duck know how close we're getting. If I write this up as anything but an accident . . ."

"How are you going to pull that off?" Chet asked.

"I'll take care of it," Trip replied. "Do you think anyone will really want to admit that our security can be breached?" Chet nodded. "I'll tell the investigating officer that I was talking to Stephen about Thelma. I'll tell them that he wanted to see something similar to the incendiary device that was used to kill her. I'll tell them I checked out a similar device. I can get the evidence people to fix the checkout dates. I'll make sure that it gets written up that Stephen was taking the device home to study when it accidentally went off. We'll say it was all an accident and that will be the public story. We'll internally flag the case." Chet didn't like the idea at all, and he didn't hide it with his expression. "I know it's risky, but right now there is someone very high up that is playing a very dangerous game. Chet you do realize that this leak, or mole, or whatever you call it has to come from a very high position?"

"Trip, how high?" Chet asked. Trip ran his hand over his bald head and looked back at the wreckage.

"Too high," he replied.

Sam's Gravesite
The Next Morning

Chapter 103

John stood over Sam's grave. He had practiced in his head what he would say all night. As he stood over her grave he began to chuckle.

"Sam what would you say to me if you knew I had practiced a speech to your gravestone?" John asked. He looked around the cemetery. He had felt like he was being watched, but he didn't see anyone; except for Jessica. That had to be what he was feeling. John continued. "Sam . . . I am so, so sorry." Tears begin to form in John's eyes. "I am sorry for taking you for granted. I am sorry . . ." John choked up and burst into tears. He sobbed for a few minutes. Jessica was standing at the car watching. She wanted to go put her arms around him, but she just didn't feel it would be appropriate. This was something John had wanted to do by himself, and she was going to honor his request.

John cried for a few minutes. As the tears dried up he looked up to the sky. The sun was trying to break through the clouds. John thought about how cliché this scene was. He burst into laughter. From her vantage point, Jessica heard the laughter and was worried. Had John finally lost it?

"Sam," John began. "I was a freaking idiot. I didn't notice you were pregnant, your friendship with Jessica, and who knows what else. Sam, I'm sorry. I'm sorry your last moments on Earth weren't happy and that was because I was too wrapped up in myself. I was too wrapped up in my problems. The alcohol didn't help matters, but I had a choice. I had a choice to be happy with you, but I chose to make my career. I chose to be the greatest FBI agent of all time. You know what that got me; loneliness."

John looked down at the ground. Tears were in his eyes, but he was composed. "Sam, I saw a therapist. I have a thingamajig. I'm not too sure how much I can trust him since he was probably on Archibald's payroll, and now he's dead, but I talked a lot of things out. Sam . . . Sam, you're dead and you're not coming back. I know I've said this before, but never to your body, here at the cemetery. Sam, I can't change what happened between us." John sunk down to his knees. "You would have been such a good Mom. I'm so sorry I never will get to find out."

John slumped his shoulders and began to cry again. He continued. "I'm going to find out who killed you, Sam, and I'm going to finish him. If it kills me, I'm going to make this right. Whoever did this is going to pay." John paused, and then sighed. "Starting this weekend, Chet, Jessica, Trip, and I are headed to your parent's house to open the case files and go over everything. I'm going to find out who did it, Sam, I promise." John placed his hand on the headstone and then began to quietly sob. After a minute or so, he collected himself and stood up. He smiled down at the tombstone.

Sam, I love you, and I always will, but it's time I let go. It's time for me to live." John looked over his shoulder at Jessica. He looked back down at the gravestone. "I think you would approve." John grinned. "Good-bye, Sam." John turned and left. He and Jessica got in the car and drove off.

After the car pulled away, a lone figure walked out of the woods. He walked up to Sam's grave and looked behind it. On the bottom of the stone, where the grass had grown over, was a microphone. Bruce reached down and took the microphone and placed it in his pocket.

"Sam," Bruce said. "I hope you miss him, because I'm about to reunite the two of you." He held out his hands and shrugged. "It's not my fault. If he would just leave this alone . . . but we both know better than that, don't we. I mean he just told you he was going to do whatever it took to find your killer and bring him to justice. I don't want justice Sam, I want what's mine. What you, my father, and John keep trying to take away from me. I want the credit I deserve." Bruce turned to leave and stopped. He turned back to the headstone. "Oh, sorry about the kid thing, I really had no idea. You realize that it's best this way. I mean, I would have had to hunt down the kid if it had been born. Clean up the bloodlines and all of that."

Bruce reached in his coat pocket and pulled out the bag that held a ring. He looked at the inscription inside and snorted. He spoke softly to himself, "If I had a sister, I wouldn't miss her." Bruce laughed and walked back to where his car had been parked in the woods.

Chapter 104

John stared out the window as the car Jessica was driving headed toward the Moores. He felt a hand squeeze his thigh right above his knee. He looked over quickly at Jessica.

"Whatcha thinking about, John?" Jessica asked.

"I'm thinking I've got to get through this weekend with Sam's parents while telling them about my worst moments as a husband. And if there are any I have forgotten, you, Trip, and Chet get to fill in any holes," John replied. Jessica grimaced at the thought.

"I'll be there with you, if it helps," Jessica said. John squeezed Jessica's hand and smiled at her.

"It will," John replied. "It will." John paused, and grinned. "Of course you have problems of your own," he said slyly. "I mean, I'm going to be telling the Moores all this, and they may be mad at you." Jessica looked at him, confused. John went on, trying to sound diplomatic. "I mean, they may think that you've replaced her since you're my new girlfriend, how," Jessica cut him off mid-sentence.

"Who says I'm your girlfriend?" she interrupted.

"I thought I just did," John replied. Jessica put both hands on the wheel and gave him a look. John had seen that look before. John thought he would never have to see that look again, but he was obviously wrong. Sam had given that look to him at least a thousand times. He thought only Sam possessed it, but he quickly realized he was wrong. Either all women possessed that look, or John had the special ability to bring it out of people. As his mind screamed at him not to ask the question on his lips, he ignored it and did so anyway. "Did I say something wrong?"

"I don't recall you ever asking me to be your girlfriend," Jessica replied, very briskly.

"Oh," John replied. He sat there not saying anything. He continued to look out the window. Jessica sat there driving. The silence became deafening. John was trying his best not to burst into laughter and to keep a straight face. The two of them traveled down the road for ten minutes in complete silence. Jessica refused to say anything, mostly on principal. Finally John spoke, very quietly.

"So, would you like to be my girlfriend?" John asked.

"Of course I would, you idiot," Jessica replied quickly. Annoyance was dripping from her voice. "I just didn't appreciate you assuming I was your girlfriend. You should have asked me. I told you we have a relationship, and I'd take it slow with you, but if you're going to start labeling things, you had best make sure all parties involved are comfortable with that label!"

"I see," John replied.

"And another thing," Jessica continued ignoring John. "Where do you get off thinking that the Moores won't like me? They love me. It was you that Arthur was so mad at!"

"I just thought with you being my girlfriend in my ex-"

"That's what you get for thinking," Jessica interjected. "Now understand this, if you start unilaterally making decisions for the two of us, John Fowler, there will be problems. You don't own me or control me. I am my own woman."

"I wouldn't dream," John began, but Jessica cut in again.

"Well don't!" She interrupted, and then paused. "Don't you have anything to say?" John took a second to think this one through.

"You're the first girlfriend I've had in a really long time," John said quietly.

Jessica looked over at John. Her lips were pursed, and her eyes were slightly squinted. She was trying to decide if he was about to feed her some line of bull or if he was being sincere. She gave him the benefit of the doubt. She looked back at the road. She spoke quietly.

"I never would try to replace her," Jessica said quietly. She looked at John. He was nodding his head. Jessica decided it had gotten too heavy, too quickly and she needed to do something to lighten the mood. "I've never had one you know."

"A boyfriend?" John asked in disbelief.

"No, silly, a girlfriend," Jessica replied smiling. John shook his head at her bad joke. The smile faded from Jessica's face as she seemed lost in deep thought. They were approaching the Moores. "I mean I don't guess you could call her one . . ." Jessica said softly. John's head whipped around in shock. Jessica was looking right at him with a "gotcha" look.

"Why do men always get so goofy when they think women did things in college?" Jessica asked.

"So you're just messing with me?" John asked. Jessica shrugged. She parked the car, leaned real close to John, and answered very softly.

"We've only been boyfriend/girlfriend for such a short time, I don't know if our relationship is strong enough to handle that yet," Jessica replied, and exited the car.

"I'm sure it is!" John cried out. The door to the Moores opened, and there was Arthur and Madeline. Jessica was standing in front of the car and turned and looked over her shoulder at John. She gave him a wink that the Moores couldn't see. She cocked her head as if to say, "Come on" and headed toward them. Madeline met her with a hug.

John opened the door and got out. He stood there for a minute and watched the three of them together. He smiled and nodded.

"Sam," he said quietly to himself. "We're going to get him . . . if it kills me we're going to get him." John shut the door and walked toward the Moores and Jessica.

The End . . . For Now.